there's something about roxy

there's something about roxy

by Madison Oaks

Based on the Characters
Created by Emily Fox
from the Motion Picture *New York Minute*

HarperEntertainment
An Imprint of HarperCollins*Publishers*

A PARACHUTE PRESS BOOK

PARACHUTE PRESS

Parachute Publishing, L.L.C.
156 Fifth Avenue
New York, NY 10010

DUALSTAR PUBLICATIONS

Dualstar Publications
1801 Century Park East
12th Floor
Los Angeles, CA 90067

HarperEntertainment
An Imprint of HarperCollins*Publishers*
10 East 53rd Street, New York, NY 10022

1

"Ladies and gentlemen! Madison Square Garden is proud to present the hottest new star in music! The one, the only . . . Roxxxxy Ryannnnn!"

Seventeen-year-old Roxanne Ryan stepped in front of her bedroom mirror, drumsticks in her hand, and struck her best rock-and-roll pose. She closed her eyes, imagining an arena filled with eager fans. Taking a deep breath, she pushed the ON button on her CD player and listened to the opening of her favorite Doll Heads track. Crisp, clean, perfect.

Eyes shut tightly, she started to drum along with the band, pounding out rhythms on her dresser, her desk, and finally moving over to her drum set.

Now she was part of the music—part of the band. Nothing except the music and the moment. Still, Roxy couldn't resist sneaking a peek at her own image in the mirror. *That's it*, she thought, shaking her wavy blond hair, furrowing her brow, and puckering her lips. *That's "the face"—the face of a rock legend.*

She topped off her drum solo with a forceful clang of the cymbal, and the fans went crazy. They chanted her name in unison, *Roxy . . . Roxy . . . Roxy . . .*

"Roxy!"

The dream seemed so real now, Roxy swore she could hear a crazed fan standing right next to her.

"Earth to Roxy! Will you *please* knock it off?"

Roxy opened her eyes and faced reality. Madison Square Garden was really her bedroom on Long Island. And the crazed fan was her twin sister, Jane, who stood in the doorway with her arms folded across her chest.

"What's up?" Roxy asked.

Jane sighed. "What's up is your drums. What is *not* up is me sleeping. Just how many solos do you plan on playing tonight? I was supposed to be on my first dream thirty-seven minutes ago."

Roxy looked at her watch. "What's the biggie, Jane? It's only nine o'clock." Then she noticed Jane was already in her pajamas. "Why are you going to bed so early anyway?"

"I'm *trying* to rest up for my day tomorrow," Jane replied.

"Tomorrow?" Roxy shot back. "Come on, all you're doing tomorrow is taking the train to Washington, D.C."

"Not exactly," Jane responded. "I've got to register at the John Adams School and pick my classes and meet the kids. This is a big deal to me, Roxy. It's the summer before senior year, and you know how much I want to get the McGill Fellowship to go to Oxford when I graduate. This program will really help me. I've got goals."

Roxy couldn't believe her ears. "Like I don't have goals?" she said, pointing to her drum set. "My friend Justin's father got me an awesome gig. Tomorrow I'll be helping the Doll Heads record their *Raw* album. Now *that's* a big deal."

"How is that going to help you get into college? Are you applying to Doll Head University?" Jane asked.

"Hey!" Roxy objected. "The Doll Heads are a major band on a major record label, and this is their first acoustic album. This is rock-and-roll history in the making, and I'll be there to help."

"How?" Jane asked. "By getting them coffee?"

Roxy shrugged. "You're just jealous."

"No, I just need a little peace and quiet," Jane replied. "Your drums are even driving Ringo nuts."

Roxy glanced at the large reptile tank sitting on her cluttered dresser. Her pet python slithered around a large rock. "Ringo loves it when I play. Don't you, baby?" she said, leaning over the tank. Then she turned back to her sister. "I hope the Addams Family School appreciates your sense of humor."

"It's the John Adams School, *not* the Addams

Family School, and it's the best precollege program in the country," Jane said. "And believe it or not, it's also going to be fun. Living on a college campus—"

"Meeting college guys?" Roxy interrupted.

"Who knows?" Jane added with a mischievous smile. "I just hope I can keep up. I want to do really well and go for that scholarship."

"Relax. You always do well," Roxy said, gesturing at her sister's perfectly pressed pj's, her perfectly scrubbed face, and her perfectly smooth hair. "So stop stressing and go to bed."

"I will," Jane replied, "as soon as you stop pounding on those drums."

"Hey, I'm not pounding. This is music." Roxy felt herself getting angry now.

"Oh, get over yourself," Jane said.

"*You* get over *your*self!" Roxy said.

A deep voice interrupted the argument. "How about you *both* get over yourselves and give *me* a break while you're at it?" Their father, Dr. Ryan, stood in the bedroom doorway glaring at them. "What's this all about?"

"Dad, Roxy won't stop playing her drums," Jane snapped, "and I need to rest up for tomorrow's trip."

Dr. Ryan gave Roxy a look, and she knew in an instant that she would lose this battle. *Jane just doesn't understand my world at all*, she thought.

"Roxy, maybe you should ease up on the drums,"

he said gently, "just for tonight. Jane will be gone for three weeks. Then you can practice all you want. Okay?"

Roxy nodded. "Fine," she said, and she flopped onto her bed as if she didn't care. "See you in three weeks, Jane."

"Works for me," Jane mumbled as she left the room.

Dr. Ryan started to close Roxy's door, but he paused for one last remark. "Try to be supportive of your sister, Rox. Tomorrow's a big day for her."

Roxy nodded her head as the door closed and her father padded down the hall. *I know tomorrow's important for Jane*, she thought. *But why can't anyone see that tomorrow's a big day for me, too? This is a huge opportunity. This is* my *future.*

She turned her head on her pillow and gazed at the glass reptile cage. Ringo slowly raised his head from beneath the rocks. "We'll show 'em, won't we, Ringo?" she whispered. "We'll show 'em that I have a future too . . . in rock-and-roll history." She closed her eyes and listened to the cheers of her adoring fans. Imaginary fans, yes. But, hey, it was a start.

By the time Roxy woke up the next morning Jane was already gone. It was just as well, Roxy figured. They both could use the following three weeks apart to cool down after last night's argument.

After dressing in jeans and a vintage Led Zeppelin T-shirt, she flew down the stairs and stopped in front of a framed picture of her mother. *This is it, Mom,* Roxy said silently. *My first big step into the music biz.* She leaned over and kissed the photograph—a ritual she and her sister performed every day.

Her mom seemed to smile back proudly, her face captured in a sunny candid shot from two years ago. In fact, it was one of the last pictures taken of her before she died.

Then Roxy turned and headed for the kitchen. She grabbed a quick bite to eat and kissed Dad's cheek before leaving for the train station.

Forty minutes on the Long Island Railroad and a subway ride later, Roxy found her way to the ultra-cool meatpacking district in lower Manhattan. The streets were paved with ancient cracked cobblestones, but most of the old buildings had been transformed into hip new boutiques, restaurants, and art galleries.

This must be the place, Roxy thought, matching the address on a slip of paper to a number on the steel door of a blocky brick warehouse. She pushed a white button and a loud buzzer unlocked the door. "Rock-and-roll history, here I come," she said.

As soon as Roxy entered the hallway, she could hear a storm of activity up on the second floor: cymbals crashing, guitars being tuned, voices shouting.

Her heart pounding, she slowly climbed the concrete stairs at the end of the hall.

Be cool, she told herself.

A young man holding a clipboard greeted her at the top of the stairs. A pencil was tucked behind his ear, and his long hair was plastered against his temples by black-framed glasses. "Oh, hi. And you are . . . ?" he asked.

"Roxy Ryan," she answered. "I'm supposed to be a production assistant."

"Ryan . . . Ryan . . . Roxy. Here you are," the young man muttered, riffling through a pile of papers. "I've got a job for you already."

"Great!" she gushed, hoping she'd get a chance to tune the band's guitars or do a sound check. "You name it."

"Coffee," the man said bluntly. "The Doll Heads need coffee. Two blacks, one light, and one cream and sugar. Think you can handle that?"

Roxy tried not to roll her eyes. "I think so," she said, hating the fact that Jane had been right about the coffee.

The young man raised an eyebrow as if he didn't believe her. "Well, the coffee cart is in the corner over here, and the band is in that room over there. Knock first."

Oh, well, Roxy thought. *You have to start somewhere.* She nodded and headed for the coffee cart, making sure to step carefully over the winding cables on the floor. Her eyes took in the whole room: a tangle of microphones and recording equipment, video cameras and lights, guitars and a drum set, all positioned in front of a spectacular view of the city's waterfront. Workers tinkered with camcorders and lights, and production assistants flitted around looking important.

Not wanting to gawk, Roxy moved on to the coffee cart and grabbed a few empty cups. Just as she was figuring out how to operate the big steel pot, someone walked up behind her.

"You new?" a girl asked. "Never seen you before."

Roxy looked up to see a pretty girl with spiky black hair, pale white skin, and large blue eyes. She was dressed all in black and, in spite of the fact that she couldn't have been much older than Roxy herself, seemed to fit here.

"Yeah," Roxy said, smiling. "Does it show that much?"

"No, it's just that you're about to give the band hot water," she pointed out. "That is the coffeepot over there." She nodded at a large chrome vat.

"Oh." Roxy turned red. "Thanks."

"No prob." The girl smiled and grabbed a cup. "Here, I'll help you. I know how the Doll Heads like their coffee. I'm a friend of the band. My name is Willow."

"Roxy," Roxy replied.

"Welcome aboard, Rox." Willow grinned. "Isn't this exciting? The Doll Heads *Raw*. Great album title, don't you think? And a great concept. Recording live in different New York locations. It's so cool. It'll give each song a different sound."

"It's brilliant," Roxy agreed. "But why the video cameras?"

"The band agreed to let RockVision film them recording for a *Raw* TV special."

Roxy's heart jumped. "You mean this will be on television?"

"Well, maybe. If you can manage to supply the band with their much-needed coffee." Willow handed Roxy a cardboard tray with four steaming cups.

"Are you kidding?" Roxy laughed. "This is what I've been waiting for. I still can't believe I'm going to meet the Doll Heads face-to-face! See you later, Willow."

I'm in the same building as the Doll Heads, she thought, crossing the loft. *This rocks. This really, truly rocks!* She stopped and once again reminded herself to be cool. *You don't want to spill coffee on them,* she thought. *That is, if you ever find them.* They weren't in the room that the guy with the glasses had indicated.

Roxy turned and froze in her tracks as a tall, balding producer type raced past, nearly knocking her over. "Everyone, stop and listen!" he shouted, and everyone in the room fell silent. "The session is canceled! The Doll Heads have left the building! Pack it up and go home."

Roxy almost dropped her tray of coffee. Her knees felt weak as his words sank in. *The Doll Heads have left? Pack it up and go home?*

"Excuse me, sir?" Roxy nervously asked the man. "What time do you want us here tomorrow?"

The producer shook his head. "I *don't* want you here tomorrow," he snapped. "As of now we're not recording *Raw*. The group just isn't ready—creative differences." The producer shook his head and walked away.

Not ready? Roxy said to herself. *Canceled? As in, my big opportunity is gone? Forever?*

"This stinks," she muttered. "This really, truly stinks."

2

Roxy stood in the middle of the studio, her mind reeling. *This can't be happening*, she thought. *The Doll Heads are gone, and so is my future. It's all over—before it even started! Why? WHY?*

She got the answer to her question when the bald producer stomped past, grumbling to an assistant, "Creative differences. Can you believe that? We drag a whole recording studio to this stupid loft, and *they* decide to have creative differences!"

"Yeah," the assistant agreed, "This was a complete waste of our time."

Roxy glumly watched the other assistants pack up the sound equipment. No band. No album. No TV special . . .

As if that wasn't depressing enough, Roxy made another awful realization: Her summer was going to be even *more* boring than Jane's!

It wasn't until the crew began leaving with their equipment that Roxy realized she was still holding the tray of coffees. Slowly she turned and moved toward the coffee cart.

"Don't look so sad," Willow said, sitting on a countertop and kicking her chunky-heeled shoes. "The Doll Heads are going through a tough time right now, that's all. They're not sure what direction to take the new album. They don't trust their own judgment anymore."

Roxy shot the girl a curious look. "How do you know all this?" she asked.

"I told you, I'm good friends with the band," Willow explained, jumping off the counter. "Their secret hideaway is right next door to the place where I crash when I go to Washington, D.C. I used to hang out with them all the time. You wouldn't believe how talkative Johnny Whisper is."

Roxy's heart jumped when she heard the lead singer's name. "Really?" she said, raising an eyebrow. "Johnny Whisper talks? Tell me more."

Willow grinned. "Well, they live on TV dinners and cheese puffs and listen to tons of classical music."

"Get out," Roxy said, excited to get the inside scoop.

"I will not," Willow insisted. "And that's not all. Their whole place is filled with plastic doll heads. Hundreds of them! Everywhere!"

Roxy felt her pulse pounding as she tried to imagine it.

"It's a killer space," Willow went on. "You should see it."

"Yes, I should," Roxy joked.

"Yes, you *should*!" Willow gasped, her big blue eyes lighting up. "I mean, really! You *should*! What a great idea!"

Roxy walked to the coffee cart and set down her tray. "What are you talking about?"

"You should see the Doll Heads' secret digs!" Willow burst out. "You and I! We could go to D.C. together, track them down, and shake them up! Really, Rox! They told me they needed fresh ears — someone young and untainted by the record industry, to listen to their new stuff."

Roxy couldn't believe what she was hearing. "That would be so amazing. I wish I could go."

Willow shook her head. "Why don't you? Johnny told me himself. He's sick and tired of stodgy old producers telling him what to play. He wants to hear from a real fan. It's perfect! You'd be great! You can stay with me and my friend."

"In Washington, D.C.?" Roxy asked.

"Yes!" Willow laughed. "There's a nine o'clock train from Penn Station tomorrow morning. Can you meet me there?"

Roxy thought fast. She *might* be able to talk her dad into it . . . somehow. It *was* a brilliant idea, wasn't it?

"Well?" Willow prompted.

Without thinking any further, Roxy gave Willow her answer. "I'll be there . . . I'll find a way. . . ."

"No," her father said that evening, barely looking up from his newspaper.

Roxy sat across from him on the sofa. "*No?* But why not?"

Dr. Ryan shook his head. "I don't know Willow, that's why not. There's no way I'm going to let you go off to Washington and stay with someone I don't know."

Roxy had expected this kind of response and was prepared with a great argument. "You let Jane go off to Washington and live stay someone you don't know."

Dr. Ryan grunted and folded his newspaper. "Roxy, that's entirely different. Jane is going to school to learn and to get ready for college. . . ."

"Listen, Dad," she went on. "Is it really so different? You let Jane go off to pursue her academic future. Well, music is *my* future. It's always been my dream, Dad. You know that better than anyone. You bought me my first drum set when I was eleven."

Dr. Ryan sighed and smiled. He was weakening. It was time for Roxy to pull out the big guns.

I hate to do this, she thought, but she took a deep breath, readying herself anyway. She had to.

"Mom would've let me go," she said softly, lowering her head. "She always encouraged me to go after my dream, no matter how crazy it seemed." It was true.

Dr. Ryan's face crumbled. "Oh, all right, honey," he gave in. "But just for a couple of days. As long as you promise to call me. And be careful. And safe. And *stay out of trouble*. And stay with Jane."

3

Trapped by her own argument, Roxy agreed to Dad's suggestion, and once Jane was assured it was only for a couple of days, she agreed too. So the next morning Dr. Ryan drove his daughter to the Long Island Railroad station and walked her to the platform. "Good luck, honey," he said.

"You're supposed to say 'Break a leg,'" Roxy reminded him. "Now you've jinxed everything."

Her father slapped his forehead. "I meant to say break a leg *and* an arm. Break everything, in fact. Break everything in sight."

Roxy shrugged. "Don't worry, Dad. I probably will."

The train arrived two minutes later. After a quick "Love you, talk to you soon," Roxy dragged her overstuffed backpack and duffel bag onto the train, nabbed a window seat, and waved good-bye to her dad on the platform. The doors closed, and the train was off.

Roxy's future had begun.

Ready or not, here I come, she thought, gazing at the world passing by her window. With each mile the train brought her closer to her destiny. Soon the Manhattan skyline came into view, and the train descended into a tunnel.

"Penn Station, next and final stop," the conductor announced over the loudspeaker.

Roxy's heartbeat quickened, her emotions racing. This was going to be great—of course there was this little problem of Jane, but she'd figure that out.

The train came to a stop, and Roxy snatched up her duffel bag and her backpack. Exiting onto the platform, she pushed her way down a corridor full of coffee shops, newsstands, and too many people. A guy selling I ♥ NEW YORK buttons tried to get her attention, but Roxy kept walking.

I'd better move it, she thought, glancing at her watch. *The train to D.C. leaves in five minutes.*

But she froze when she heard a girl scream. "No! Stop! Somebody help me!"

It sounded like Willow!

She spun around quickly and spotted the spiky-haired girl running away from a tall man wearing a pair of sunglasses, which had lenses that reflected like mirrors. Willow shouted at him loudly, but the man didn't give up.

"Get away!" Willow cried.

Roxy knew she had to do something—fast!

Roxy charged at the man and swung her duffel bag as hard as she could. With a loud thud it smashed into the back of the man's legs, buckling his knees and bringing him down.

"Run for it!" Willow shouted, waving Roxy toward the main hall of Penn Station.

The two girls dashed into a swarming crowd of morning commuters.

Willow stopped in the middle and looked around. "I have our tickets." She gasped. "The train leaves on track nine . . . any second!"

Roxy scanned the archways and pointed to the left. "This way!"

The girls turned to run but froze when they saw the man with the mirror shades standing in their path.

"We've got to lose him." Willow reached for Roxy's hand, and they circled around the crowd.

Roxy stumbled forward, her duffel banging into one annoyed commuter after another. "Sorry . . . excuse me . . . sorry about that, sir," she apologized as the pair zigzagged their way across Penn Station. Roxy peeked over her shoulder.

The man was right behind them.

"Hurry!" Roxy cried. Turning fast and stumbling through gate nine, Roxy and Willow charged down the platform toward the train.

"All aboard!" the conductor announced.

The girls made a mad dash for the door, Willow jumping aboard first with Roxy crashing in through the doors behind her.

A few feet back the man in the sunglasses lunged and dove after them, but the doors closed in his face. The man screamed something, but Roxy couldn't tell what he was saying.

Willow and Roxy cheered as the train started to move. Gasping with relief, Roxy looked back at their pursuer. The man lowered his glasses and locked eyes with her, sending a creepy chill up her spine. What did he want from them? Why had he chased them?

But Willow didn't seem nearly as freaked as Roxy was. "Buh-bye," she crooned, waving.

The man glared back at them from the platform, huffing and puffing from exertion. Seconds later the train plunged into the darkness of a tunnel, and he disappeared from view.

"Way to go, Rox! You kicked butt!" Willow burst out, high-fiving her new friend and pointing to a pair of empty seats.

Roxy slid her duffel into an overhead compartment and flopped into her seat. "So who was that guy?" she asked Willow.

Willow shrugged. "I don't know. Maybe he wanted my wallet, or maybe he thought I was someone else. I wasn't going to stick around to find out."

Roxy was a bit surprised by how calm Willow seemed about the whole thing. "Shouldn't we call the police or dial 911 or something?"

"Cell phones won't work inside this tunnel," Willow said. "Anyway, we'll be in D.C. soon, and I'm sure that guy is long gone by now so what would be the point? Hey, what's on your T-shirt?"

Roxy glanced down at her shirt. "Just some lint."

"No, I mean, what band?"

"Oh." Roxy laughed. "The Who. Doesn't get any better than that."

Soon the girls were babbling on about their favorite bands and music videos and radio stations. Roxy learned that Willow had lots of friends in the record industry and that she loved all kinds of music, even classical and jazz. As they talked, Roxy pulled her drumsticks out of her bag and drummed softly on her lap.

"You're pretty good with those sticks," Willow said with a smile. "You seem so comfortable."

"I love to play, but I get frustrated sometimes," Roxy explained. "I wish I could play what's inside my head. You should hear me in my dreams."

"If you can dream it, Rox, you can do it," Willow said.

Roxy smiled. "That's what *I* always say!"

The hours flew by, and, before they knew it, the train had reached their destination. Willow and Roxy grabbed their stuff, stepped off the train, and headed into the cavernous main hall of Union Station.

"Beautiful," Roxy commented, gazing up at the tall white columns and vaulted ceiling.

Willow swiftly forged ahead to the taxi stand and hailed a cab while Roxy stood there gawking. "Come on, Rox! Let's go!"

Roxy wondered why Willow was in such a rush but didn't say anything. Hurrying to the curb, she crawled into the cab and hauled her duffel across her lap, reminding herself to call Jane. Willow told the driver an address and soon they were off, zooming past the Washington Monument and the Capitol and other landmarks Roxy had seen on TV. But then the gleaming landscape of government buildings gave way to a bleaker urban terrain. Old brick tenements and bargain stores lined the streets.

"Are we leaving the city?" Roxy asked.

"No. Just going to a different part," Willow explained. "It's not far."

Roxy's plan was to check in with Jane, but she was sure Jane wouldn't mind if she stayed with Willow some of the time. Roxy figured Willow lived in a really cool part of town, but as she gazed out her window, the view got worse and worse. All she could see was row after row of crumbling warehouses and an abandoned gas station or two. Her stomach flip-flopped while a mix of emotions flooded her mind.

On the one hand she was thrilled: She was going to meet the Doll Heads! On the other hand she was worried about Dad's warnings: Just who was Willow and where was she taking her?

"Here we are," the cab driver grunted, coming to a sudden stop. "You sure this is the right address?"

Roxy wondered the same thing. She looked out the window at a giant gray cinder-block building.

"This is it," Willow chirped, paying the driver and climbing out of the cab. "What do you think, Rox?"

Roxy dragged her stuff to the curb, gazing up at the grim warehouse with disbelief. "It's very . . . industrial."

"Yeah, cool, huh?" Willow grinned, walking toward the building's huge steel door.

Roxy hesitated. She tried to tell herself that everything was cool: She was going to hang out in a hip loft space and jam with the Doll Heads. What could be cooler?

Noticing Roxy's hesitation, Willow chimed in, "You're not worried about the neighborhood, are you? It's not as dangerous as it looks. See those ivy-covered buildings over there?"

Roxy looked down the street and nodded.

"That's the John Adams School."

"The John Adams School? Right down the street?"

Willow tilted her head. "Yeah, why? Are you thinking of taking some classes? They have a killer precollege program."

"Yes, I know," Roxy grumbled. "That's where my sister is right now."

"Oh, that's cool . . . isn't it?" Willow asked.

Roxy shrugged. "I knew Jane was somewhere here in D.C., but I didn't expect her to be just one block away. I mean, I love my sister—but this summer was supposed to be my big chance to prove myself. On my own."

Willow set down her bag. "Listen," she said, throwing an arm around Roxy's shoulders, "I'm not easily impressed by people, believe me. But . . . well, there's something about you, Rox. I don't know what or why, but I think you're just what the Doll Heads need."

"Maybe it's the way I swing a duffel bag," Roxy joked.

"You bet," Willow added. "Roxy, you have style to burn."

Roxy stared at the ivy-covered school buildings, then looked Willow in the eye. "Thanks for the pep talk," she said.

"Hey, it's what I do." Willow laughed. "And don't worry. You'll get your chance to prove yourself. You are going to rock the house."

"Speaking of which," Roxy said, glancing at all

the warehouses, "which one is the Doll Heads' place?"

Willow pointed to an abandoned-looking factory next door. "That's it. But first let's settle in and grab something to eat." She pushed a button on the warehouse intercom and waited. Seconds later the door opened with a loud buzz.

Roxy stepped inside and gasped.

The place was totally empty—nothing but a sprawling dark space with dirty concrete floors and a single bare lightbulb.

"I don't understand," Roxy mumbled. "What is this place?"

Her father's warning rang inside her head: *Be safe . . . stay out of trouble. . . .*

Then the door slammed shut behind her.

And the light went out.

4

What is this? Roxy wondered nervously. *Some sort of trap? Have I been set up? Where's Willow?*

She squinted but couldn't see a thing.

She was alone. In the dark.

"Willow? *Willow!*" Roxy's voice echoed in the pitch-black room. "Where are you? What's going on?"

"I'm over here," Willow said from a far corner. She flicked on a lighter and smiled. "The bulb must have burned out. Come on, Rox. The loft is upstairs," she explained, nodding at a nearby freight elevator. "Your chariot awaits."

Roxy sighed with relief, feeling a little silly for being so nervous. She climbed aboard the elevator, hoping that Willow didn't notice how spooked she really was.

Willow stepped in after her, closed the door, and pulled a huge lever. With a jolt the steel cage started rising.

Roxy peered through the chain-link walls as the

elevator rumbled upwards past each gloomy floor.

When they reached the top, Willow announced, "Sixth floor. Men's briefs and ladies' undergarments."

Roxy laughed but wasn't very happy with what she saw. This floor didn't look any better than the first. A dull metal clip-on lamp hung from a brown exposed beam, casting a long shadow across a bleak, empty hallway.

Roxy thought it looked like the dead end of a sewer. But then she spied a clean white wall to her left and a wooden door with an ABBEY ROAD sign on it.

"Scratch!" Willow shouted out. "Scratch!"

Just then the wooden door swung open, and a tall, scruffy boy with a goatee held out his arms. "Hey! How's it going?"

Willow gave her friend a huge hug, then waved Roxy inside.

Stepping carefully over a pile of newspapers, Roxy did a quick scan of the room. The walls were plastered with concert posters, the floor was littered with Chinese take-out containers, and the only furniture was a single mattress in the corner.

Well, it's not The Plaza, Roxy thought. *But it's kind of cool in a grunge-rock sort of way.*

"Roxy, this is Scratch," Willow said, introducing her friend.

Roxy smiled and said hi. "I like your posters," she added.

Scratch started to point out his favorites when Willow interrupted. "Sorry, Scratch, but Roxy and I need to eat. Desperately. You two talk while I slip into something less comfortable. Then we'll hit the corner diner." She picked up her bag and went into the next room.

"Check out the view," Scratch suggested, pointing to a wall of large windows. "You can see the Washington Monument from here. Sort of."

Roxy leaned forward and squinted. "Where?"

"See that tiny triangle of white peeping over that warehouse? That's it."

Roxy nodded, then lowered her gaze to a grass square surrounded by ivy-covered buildings. "Is that the John Adams School?"

Scratch smirked. "Yeah. I call it Prep Central."

Roxy nodded. *Jane will probably love it*, she thought. *Classes, clubs, cultural events, preppy clothes, and squeaky-clean dorm rooms.* She studied the old mattress on the floor. *I guess clean sheets wouldn't be so bad.* Then she glanced from the garbage on the floor to the pristine lawn of the school in the distance. *But, hey*, she told herself, *Scratch's place is about as rock-and-roll as you can get . . . without being condemned by the Department of Sanitation.*

Roxy was about to ask Scratch another question about the school when Willow burst into the room.

"Ta-da! How do I look?" she asked, striking a

pose. She wore pink sandals, orange capri pants, and a pink sleeveless blouse—all topped off with a short pink wig.

Roxy was almost speechless. "You look . . . well, pink!" she managed to say.

"So true," Willow said, slipping on a pair of cat's-eye sunglasses. "Let's bust."

The diner was a little run-down, with its vintage bar stools and vinyl booths, but the food was delicious. Roxy practically inhaled her grilled cheese sandwich while Willow gobbled down a salad and fries.

As soon as the waitress brought the check, Roxy pulled money from her pocket and laid it on the table. "Ready to go?"

"What's the rush?" Willow asked, still picking at her salad.

Roxy glanced nervously at the door. "I really should call my sister," she explained. "I promised my dad. . . ."

"I'm sure she's hanging out at John Adams with her new buddies," Willow said. "I know people in that program. They keep them pretty busy over there. They're high energy—if you know what I mean."

"High energy. That's Jane. I'll bet she's having the time of her life," Roxy said, starting to relax. "And anyway, I can call her later."

Willow looked up from her iced tea—and her jaw dropped.

Confused, Roxy glanced behind her and saw Jane stroll into the diner. She gasped and quickly ducked under the table.

"Rox?" Willow asked. "What are you doing under there? Looking for gum?"

"No. Look over there," Roxy whispered. "That's my sister."

Willow leaned forward. "Yeah," she said, "I noticed. Couldn't help it. She looks just like you. Though I must say, I think she shops in a different universe than you do. She's wearing a beige blazer and skirt with a white shirt."

"That's Jane." Roxy sighed. "I don't want her to think I'm avoiding her. What's she doing in a place like this?"

"I'm not a mind reader, but she probably came to eat," Willow said.

Roxy peeked over the tabletop. "What's she doing now?"

Willow reported on what she saw. "She's chatting with a preppy-looking girl and a cute guy. Now the waitress is seating them at a booth by the door."

"Great," Roxy moaned. She didn't want to run into her sister like this. "I've got to get out of here."

"Wait. She's standing up," Willow said. "And she's heading this way . . . with a packet of hand wipes?"

Roxy lowered her head and held her breath as Jane walked swiftly past her table.

"You can relax now," Willow informed her. "She went into the bathroom. Let's go."

"I can't," Roxy said. "I'll have to walk past her friends, and if they see me, they'll know for sure I'm her sister."

"I have an idea," Willow whispered. "Here." She removed her pink wig and cat's-eye sunglasses and passed them under the table.

"Willow, you're brilliant." Roxy tucked her hair into the wig and slipped on the shades. "Let's roll."

The two girls stood up and sauntered to the entrance. Roxy couldn't resist checking out Jane's new friends. As she passed their booth, the dark-haired boy suddenly glanced up from his menu and smiled at her. His deep brown eyes and dazzling grin nearly stopped Roxy in her tracks.

Willow's right, she thought. *He* is *cute*. Very *cute*.

Roxy felt a tug on her arm. "Let's go, Peggy Sue," Willow urged, pulling her out the door and into the street.

Roxy stumbled to the sidewalk, giggling. "Peggy Sue?"

"Well, I couldn't use your real name, could I?"

"Yes, but . . . Peggy Sue? Do I look like a Peggy Sue in this wig?"

Willow squinted at Roxy and laughed. "No, you

look more like an overgrown action hero doll."

When they turned the corner, Roxy pulled off the wig and handed it back to Willow. "I'm flattered, but I think it looks better on you."

Willow tucked her hair into the wig. "Well, if you need another disguise, I have a whole box of these things back at the loft."

"Really? Why?"

"So I won't be recognized by all my adoring fans, of course." Willow fluttered her eyelashes like a Hollywood starlet.

Roxy laughed. She couldn't believe how much fun she was having—in spite of her recent near-Jane experience. "Jane. I really do have to call Jane soon. I don't want her to worry," she said.

"Call her now," Willow said. "Leave a message at her dorm right now! We know she's not there!"

"Willow, you are a genius," Roxy said. "I'll tell her I'll see her tomorrow."

After making the call and leaving Jane a message, Roxy smiled and said, "What's next on our agenda?"

Willow didn't skip a beat. "Let's go hang with the Doll Heads," she said, stopping and pointing up at the old brick factory behind them.

Roxy's stomach flipped. "Really? Now? But . . . should we warn them first? Should I change my clothes?"

Willow rolled her eyes. "Well, we *could* go back to

the loft, send them a telegram, and wait around in our fancy evening gowns. Or we could just do this." She marched up to the factory entrance and pushed the buzzer.

"Willow, are you sure this is okay?" Roxy wasn't usually so nervous, but this was the Doll Heads! Oh, well. No one answered the door anyway. "Maybe they're not home," she said.

"Let's go around back," Willow suggested, leading Roxy down a long narrow alley to a set of darkened windows.

"They're too high to see into," Roxy said, wondering what the Doll Heads' secret loft looked like. If she could just get a peek . . .

"Give me a boost, Willow," she said, even though something told her this wasn't exactly the way to stay out of trouble. "I just want to get a quick look, then we'll come back later. Okay?"

"Your wish is my command," Willow said, bowing her head. She bent over and leaned against the building for support.

Roxy climbed up onto her back.

"Ow! Easy with those heels, spy girl," Willow said.

"Sorry!" Roxy pulled herself up to a window, pressed her face to the dirty glass, and sighed. "I can't see a thing. I'm coming down . . . before we get into trouble."

Then she heard something behind her. Quick footsteps.

"What are you girls doing?" a man shouted.

Roxy gulped. *Too late*, she thought. *We* are *in trouble!*

5

God, how embarrassing, Roxy thought, not turning to face the guy. "Oh, we were just . . . spying?" Roxy said, trying to sound light and funny as she slid to the ground. She hoped it would work.

It did. The man burst out laughing.

Willow squealed. "Johnny! I knew you'd be here!"

Roxy turned around and found herself face-to-face with Johnny Whisper, lead singer and guitarist of the Doll Heads. At first she couldn't believe it, but there he was—lanky arms and legs, buzz cut, and all. *The* Johnny Whisper.

"Johnny, meet Roxy," Willow said with a smile. "She's a budding musical talent, a huge fan of yours, *and* she's not connected to the record industry."

Roxy's stomach flipped when Johnny looked at her. *Don't freak*, she told herself.

Johnny's famous green eyes lit up. "Nice to meet you, Roxy. Excellent spying skills," he said in a charm-

34

ing growl. "Hey, we're rehearsing some new stuff right now. You guys want to come in and listen?"

Roxy felt like she was about to faint. "Ah, sure," she answered.

Johnny led the girls to the front of the factory, threw open a pair of doors, and ushered them into a massive sunlit hall with polished wood floors and hundreds of plastic doll heads hanging from the ceiling. In the middle of it all was a cluster of guitars, drums, keyboards, and something even more amazing: the rest of the band.

I'm here, Roxy thought. *I'm actually here!* She tried hard not to act *too* star struck as she was introduced, to the Doll Heads one by one: Sneaky Pete, the keyboardist, Jones, the bass player, and everyone's favorite drummer, Face. They all seemed happy to meet her.

"We could use a pair of fresh ears," Johnny told Roxy. "We've rehearsed our new stuff so many times and so many ways, we don't know what sounds good anymore."

"I'd *love* to hear it," Roxy said, hardly believing her luck. As the band prepared to play, Roxy stared down at Face's drum set.

"Do you play?" Face asked, noticing her interest.

"Sort of," she answered.

"Come on over here—try my sticks," he said. "Go for it."

Roxy smiled sheepishly and sat down behind the snare. *This can't be happening*, she thought. *It's a dream come true!*

Roxy took a deep breath. *Calm down, Rox. Just concentrate, and you'll do fine. . . .* Closing her eyes, she tried to imagine she was back in her bedroom playing for her pet snake, Ringo. She tapped out an easy rhythm on the snare. Face answered the rhythm with a syncopated beat on the conga.

Johnny picked up his guitar and played the beginning of "Stairway to Heaven."

Roxy was so shocked, she dropped a drumstick. "I never said I was *good*." She smiled weakly.

Sneaky Pete shrugged. "Hey, we all have to start somewhere."

"And I think we all started with 'Stairway to Heaven,'" Jones added.

Everyone laughed.

"I'll be honest with you, Roxy," Johnny said with a smile. "That rendition of 'Stairway' doesn't sound any worse than the new song we're working on. Am I right, guys?"

The rest of the band groaned and nodded.

"Oh, come on," Roxy protested. She didn't believe him, but she appreciated his attempt to make her feel better.

"Listen for yourself," Johnny said, reaching for a different guitar.

The rest of the band strapped up to play.

"Okay, Face, give us a beat," Johnny said. "One, two, three, four . . ."

Johnny jumped in with a killer guitar riff, echoed by Jones on bass. Then Pete snuck into the mix on keyboards.

Roxy tilted her head and listened. The music was totally different from the band's hit songs. More atmospheric and moody. It was interesting, but it just didn't grab you the way their music usually did.

After a short chorus Johnny waved an arm and the band stopped playing. "It's just too slow, man," Johnny said to Face.

"Slow," Steady Pete repeated. "It's just weak. It needs more juice."

The band argued back and forth, and after a pause, Johnny said, "Roxy, what do you think?"

Roxy chose her words carefully. "It's very . . . unusual but definitely original. It sounds almost classical . . . in a strange way."

A broad smile spread over Johnny's face. "I'm classically trained," he told her. "I started out as a violinist."

"Really?" Roxy replied, too embarrassed to tell him she already knew that from a fan magazine she had read. "Well, I think mixing classical and rock is a great idea, but it needs something."

"Like what?" Johnny asked, his eyebrows raised.

Roxy was surprised by his intense interest. *He really seems to care what I think*, she realized with a start.

"It needs . . . I don't know . . . a stronger backbeat maybe? You know, something to pump it up," Roxy tried to explain. Her eyes scanned the room, stopping at a cymbal on the floor. "Like this." She picked up the cymbal and a stray drumstick and started banging it out.

Ding-ding, ding-ding-ding.

Roxy clanged with all the energy and enthusiasm she could muster.

Johnny's jaw dropped open. "Roxy, that's great!" he shouted. "Don't stop! Keep it up!"

Ding-ding, ding-ding-ding!

"Come on, guys! Jump in!" Johnny said.

Face supplied a cool counter beat on drums, while Johnny and Jones gave it a classical spin with their guitars. Sneaky Pete's keyboards joined in and the sound just clicked.

Then Johnny began to sing, sweeping Roxy into the moment.

The band was rocking. Hard.

And Roxy was in rock-and-roll heaven!

"What a day! What a band! What an experience!" Roxy burst into the loft that night and flopped down onto the mattress. "I don't know how I'm going to sleep."

Willow looked down, shaking her head. "You're not tired out from bashing a mugger, ducking your sister, and jamming with your favorite band? I don't know what kind of energy drink you're on, but I'm exhausted."

With that, Willow retired to the spare bedroom, leaving Roxy alone with her thoughts.

Humming and smiling, she pushed the empty take-out containers off the mattress. *Even garbage can't spoil my excitement,* she thought. Turning off the light, she lay back, closed her eyes, and tried to go to sleep.

She sniffed the air. *Ew! What is that stench? Is it coming from the mattress?* She smelled the bed. It was! *Jane would have a heart attack if she had to sleep here,* Roxy thought with a laugh.

She pulled a sweatshirt out of her backpack and laid it on the mattress to block the bad smell. But it still reeked.

Maybe I should move. Roxy glanced at the floor, but it seemed even dirtier than the mattress.

Okay, so the place was a dump. So what? She didn't need a fancy school to make her dreams come true like Jane did. This was the real world. This was rock and roll.

Something rustled next to the mattress.

Did one of those food containers move? she asked herself.

She lifted her head and looked. Nothing.

Roxy lay back and closed her eyes again—

Until she felt something furry moving around next to her head.

Something *alive*! Gross!

6

The next morning Roxy awoke to the sound of voices and the smell of coffee brewing. She quickly changed clothes, grabbed her backpack and duffel, and headed to the kitchen.

"Look who's awake," Scratch said, glancing up from his morning paper.

Willow, wearing a long, straight, blond wig, smiled at Roxy and asked, "So you finally fell asleep, huh?"

Roxy yawned. "Yeah, finally. Sorry about all the screaming last night."

"I'm sorry about the mice," Scratch replied. "I guess I should clean up those Chinese take-out cartons."

"You think?" Willow asked with a raised eyebrow.

Scratch shrugged and rubbed his goatee thoughtfully. "What are you girls doing today?"

Willow started to answer, but Roxy interrupted. "I have to see Jane today," she told them. "I think maybe I'll crash there tonight."

"The mice. I knew it," Scratch mumbled.

"It's not that," Roxy explained. Well, maybe that *was* a reason, but she wasn't about to tell Scratch that. He was a good guy and she didn't want to hurt his feelings. "My dad wants me to stay with my sister. You know, family stuff. They worry about me."

"I can set traps," Scratch offered, not buying it. "Or get a cat."

Roxy laughed and gave him a mock slap. "Believe me, I wish I could stay here longer," she said. "I'd love to jam with the Doll Heads again . . . and hang with you guys, of course."

"That can be arranged," Willow said sweetly.

"Oh, yeah." Roxy smirked. "I think I've found my calling. Roxy Ryan, cymbal girl."

"No, really," Willow insisted. "Girl, you got rhythm!"

Roxy blushed and gave her a hug. "Thanks for everything, Willow. I'll talk to you tonight. And, Scratch, you're the host with the most."

"The most mice." Scratch grunted. "Are you sure you're not leaving because of the mice?"

"Oh, please," Roxy answered. "Those pip-squeaks would be no match for my python, Ringo."

Scratch scanned the room nervously. "You, uh, didn't bring him along, did you?"

"Next time," she answered, turning for the door. "Later, guys!"

"Roxy! Wait!" Willow ran after her with an orange flyer in her hand. "Here. I forgot to give you this."

Roxy examined the flyer. The words *A Very Special Party* were printed over a picture of a television set with a slash through it.

"It's an invitation to a private party tonight. The Doll Heads are making a surprise appearance, so the location is a secret. Just go to the corner marked here on the map and someone will tell you where the party is."

"Awesome. I'll see you tonight then." Roxy gave her friend another hug and headed outside. The warm summer air felt good and, best of all, smelled wonderful. *From garbage to Jane,* she thought. *What a trip.*

Five minutes later she arrived at the John Adams School. The campus sat in the middle of the warehouse district like a castle in a junkyard. Its classic colonial buildings were adorned with English ivy and tall white columns, and the large green lawn was perfectly manicured.

Roxy felt a little underdressed as she carried her duffel past a small group of students. Preppy was obviously the style of choice here. A couple of girls stared curiously at Roxy's black Ramones T-shirt and short denim skirt.

"Excuse me," she asked them. "Could you tell me where the girls' dorm is?"

The girls smiled and pointed to a building at a far corner of the campus. Roxy thanked them and made a beeline for the dorm, stepping off the pavement and onto the lawn. She practically tripped on a sign that said: PLEASE STAY OFF THE GRASS.

"Oops." Roxy hopped back onto the pavement. *It figures*, she thought.

Reaching the girls' dorm, she pulled a slip of paper out of her backpack and double-checked Jane's address and room number. Then, taking a deep breath, she opened the heavy wooden door and marched boldly across the lobby.

"Excuse me!" spouted a gray-haired woman behind a large reception desk.

Roxy stopped and faced her.

"Did you lose your ID?" the woman asked.

Roxy stammered. "Well, um, yes. Silly me," she told her. "Do you have my spare? I'm Jane Ryan."

The woman smiled warmly and opened a desk drawer. "Here it is, Jane. Good thing you made a copy."

Roxy smiled. She *knew* Jane would have a duplicate ID. After all, she had three copies of her library card, two spare Blockbuster cards, and six extra high school IDs—even though Jane *never* misplaced *anything*.

The woman handed Roxy a laminated ID card and gave her an odd little wink. Roxy wasn't sure if it was a real wink or just a twitch, but she winked back anyway. Then, turning to a large staircase, she bounded up the steps two at a time and headed down the hall. Everything was tastefully decorated with beige walls and white trim. A few girls said "Hi, Jane," though they seemed confused by Roxy's outfit. Laughing to herself, she found room 2D and flung the door open. "I'm here!" she announced.

A girl with long straight red hair and thick glasses looked up from her laptop. Roxy recognized her from the diner.

"Oh, hi, Jane," the girl said flatly. "Cool T-shirt. When did you get that?"

Roxy figured she'd better explain. "I'm not Jane. I'm her sister, Roxy . . . making a surprise visit."

The girl blushed, her face almost matching her red hair. "Oh, I-I'm sorry," she stammered. "I'm Betsy, her roommate. Jane isn't here now. She's at a meeting for the school's benefit concert. But she should be back—oh, here she is now!"

Roxy spun around, ready to greet her sister with a smile and a hug. But she scrapped that plan when she saw Jane's face.

"You were supposed to call me yesterday," Jane said, standing in the doorway with a pretty brunette and the cute boy from the diner.

Roxy gulped and decided to forge ahead with her story. "I know, but you're *not* going to believe this!

Remember the gig I had with the Doll Heads? Well, here's what happened. . . ."

Ignoring the disapproval in Jane's eyes, she rambled on and on without stopping. As she told her story, she had trouble keeping her eyes off the boy, who was even hotter than she had realized at the diner!

A huge grin spread across his face when she rattled off the details about Willow and her wigs, the Doll Heads and their secret factory, and even Scratch and his mouse problem. She did, however, leave out the part about the man with the sunglasses at Penn Station, not wanting to alarm Jane.

She'd probably tell Dad, too, Roxy thought.

She finished her story, and everyone seemed impressed—especially the cutie.

"Oh, man!" he gushed. "I can't believe you got to play with the Doll Heads!"

"Well, just a cymbal," Roxy admitted, looking him in the eye.

"*Just* a cymbal?" he said with twinkling smile. "Are you kidding? Some of the greatest musicians in the world played the cymbal. Mozart, Beethoven, Bach . . . all *brilliant* cymbal players."

"Really? I didn't know that." Roxy tried to hold back her laughter.

"It's a fact," he went on. "The cymbal takes only seconds to learn but a lifetime to master."

"Maybe," Roxy said, grinning. "Let me guess. You're on the debating team, am I right?"

"You are right," he said, flashing major dimples. "My name's Rafael, by the way, and this is my cousin, Claire."

"Hello and hello." Roxy waved with both hands.

"Welcome to the Roxy Show," Jane added dryly. "Enter at your own risk."

Everyone laughed at Jane's joke, but Roxy wasn't amused.

"Jane and I kid each other all the time," Roxy explained. "But we're actually very close. In fact, I was just going to ask Jane if she'd let me crash here tonight. It'll be so much fun, won't it, sis?"

Jane pressed her lips together tightly. Roxy could almost see steam bubbling out of her ears.

"That would be great!" Rafael jumped in before Jane could answer. "You can come to brunch tomorrow at my parents' house. There'll be a lot of Washington stuffed shirts there, but it could be fun."

"Tomorrow?" Roxy asked, thrilled with the invitation.

Cute and *friendly*, she thought. *I like that in a guy.*

"Oh, Roxy is probably too busy," Jane chimed in. "Aren't you rehearsing with the Doll Heads tomorrow?"

"Oh, they sleep in till noon," Roxy shot back, adding, "I'd love to have brunch, Rafael."

The boy's handsome face lit up. "Excellent. Jane can give you the details. She's coming too."

Rafael looked at his watch, then his cousin. "Well, Claire and I have a class to catch now. See you later." He smiled, and the two of them left the room.

"I'm going, too," Jane's roommate, Betsy, said. "I need to hit the library. And I'm sure you two have lots to talk about." With that, Betsy slipped out of the room, closing the door behind her.

The sisters were finally alone. At first neither spoke or even moved. At least Jane wasn't freaking out, which was a good sign. Roxy hoped everything was cool between them.

"Roxy, you know I love you," Jane said. "Like a sister."

Roxy smiled.

"But you're not going to that brunch," Jane went on. "And you're not staying here either!"

7

It took a second for Jane's words to sink in. And when they finally did, Roxy was furious.

"Why not, Jane?" she asked. "You told Dad I could stay."

Jane took a deep breath. "Look, Roxy," she began, "I understand how psyched you are to be hanging out with the Doll Heads. It's a big opportunity for you. But we'll just be too on top of each other."

"I won't get in the way . . ." Roxy began.

Jane cut her off, pacing back and forth as she spoke. "The academic program here is *really* tough— was harder that anything I've done before. And I *really* need to impress my advisor so I can score a recommendation for the McGill Fellowship I'm applying for in the fall."

Roxy's anger faded when she saw how stressed out her sister was. "Jane, I know you're under a lot of pressure. But I also know that you're a killer student, and you're going to kick butt all across campus."

Jane smiled weakly and collapsed onto her bed. "Thanks, Roxy, but it's not the academics I'm worried about. This place is very artsy. The faculty wants us to be well rounded in everything . . . music, art, dance, you name it. That's why I joined the the Music Club. And that's why I want you to skip that brunch tomorrow."

"Huh?" Roxy was confused.

Jane sat up. "Rafael is having his parents throw this brunch to lure in sponsors for the Music Club's benefit concert this weekend. His parents are Washington hotshots, and it's my job, as the concert organizer, to hit up their political friends for funding."

"I still don't get it," Roxy said, cutting in. "Why can't I go?"

Jane sighed. "Because you'll bring a python or wear a pink wig or play 'Stairway to Heaven' on the bagpipes or *something* weird. Face it. There's something about you, Roxy. And whatever it is usually turns everything into total chaos."

Roxy sat on the bed. "That's funny," she said. "Willow told me the same thing. But she meant it as a compliment."

For a moment both girls remained quiet. Then a muffled beeping sound broke the silence.

"Your backpack is ringing," Jane pointed out.

"Oh." Roxy jumped up and dug through her backpack until she found her cell phone. "Hello?"

"So how's my rock star?" Dad asked.

"Dad! Hi! I'm great! I'm here with Jane at the Addams Family School." She held the phone in front of Jane's face. "Say hi to Dad."

"Hi to Dad," Jane said sweetly.

Roxy brought the phone back to her ear. "You're not going to believe this, Dad, but I got to jam with the Doll Heads! They tried out their new songs on me and asked what I thought."

"Wow, that's terrific," Dr. Ryan remarked. "I guess this means you don't want to come home tomorrow."

Roxy winced. "Well, I was hoping I could stay here a little longer," she admitted, glancing at Jane nervously. "The Doll Heads are playing at a private party tonight, and Jane is taking me to a brunch for the Music Club tomorrow, and I'm having *soooo* much fun. Can I stay? *Pleeease?*"

Knowing she needed her sister's permission as much as her dad's, Roxy gave Jane a long, pleading look.

Jane sighed, shrugged, and finally nodded.

Roxy let out a silent cheer and danced a little dance, then continued her assault on her father. "Please, Dad. I'll stay here with Jane."

"For how long?" he asked.

"How long?" Roxy repeated the question, glancing back at Jane. "I'm thinking . . . maybe through the weekend?"

Once again she gave her sister a pleading look. And once again Jane nodded yes.

"Okay," her dad agreed.

"All right!" Roxy shouted. "You rule, Dad! I promise you won't regret it. I'll call you soon, okay? Love you!"

She clicked the phone shut and jumped on top of Jane, bombarding her with thank-you hugs and bouncing on the bed. Finally she flopped down beside her sister. "Look, Jane. I promise I won't get in your way. I *promise*. And I'll help you out in any way I can," she said.

Jane tilted her head, gazing at Roxy with a strange, thoughtful expression. "Do you think you could help me with some of the more artsy and creative things?" she asked.

"Of course," Roxy answered, touched by her sister's request.

Then a sly smile crept over Jane's face. "And do you think you could help me make this bed again? You messed it all up."

Roxy rolled her eyes. Some things never change.

Later that morning the dorm's gray-haired receptionist looked up from her desk and smiled at the sisters as they passed through the lobby. "Hi, girls," she said, pulling off her glasses and winking.

Roxy winked back.

"Don't do that," Jane whispered. "She has a nervous tic. She winks that way all the time."

"Oops," Roxy whispered back. "I thought she liked me."

They stumbled, giggling, into the hot sunlight and headed across campus. "Isn't it beautiful?" Jane said. "It's like a college preview."

"The dorm is cool," Roxy added. "And no mice. What's all this?" she asked, pointing to a bunch of colorful booths on the edge of the lawn.

"Oh, those are the sign-up booths for all the clubs and activities," Jane explained. "That's where I joined the Music Club. Why don't you check them out while I go to my economics lecture? See if there's anything else that seems interesting."

"Okay," Roxy agreed, intrigued by the idea.

"Remember, I'm looking for something artsy," Jane reminded her. "But not *too* artsy. No Belly Dancers of America. Got it?"

Roxy smirked. "Oh, come on. Don't you trust me, sis?"

"No comment," Jane replied, stopping in front of the Office of Business Management and glancing at her watch. "Okay, I'm off to class now. Have fun, and grab yourself some lunch while you're at it. See you back in my dorm room in two hours and fifteen . . . no, fourteen minutes." She turned and entered the building.

Alone, Roxy surveyed the campus. Students roamed back and forth between buildings, talking and laughing, and Roxy had to admit they weren't all as preppy as she'd first thought. In fact, most of the kids seemed pretty cool.

She sauntered along the edge of the lawn, eyeing all the sign-up booths. She was pleasantly surprised by the interesting selection: the Tennis Club, the New Film Club, the Stand-Up Comedy League, the Theater Troop, the Chess Enthusiasts, and a Web Design Club.

"What's this?" Roxy murmured, stopping in front of a particularly eye-catching booth. A large sign spelled out *The Underground Dance Music Club* in psychedelic letters. A purple strobe light flickered next to a stack of sample CDs, and a placard featured glossy photos of bands and clubs and mobs of hip young dancers.

Roxy studied the brightly colored party flyers spread across the countertop. Then she noticed who was manning the booth. It was that cutie, Rafael. *Hmm*, she thought. *There's more to this guy than just preppy clothes.* Without hesitation she pulled out her sister's ID, slapped it down onto the counter, and said, "I'm in. Sign me up."

"Hey, Roxy," he said, smiling that killer smile of his. "What's up?"

"Oh, I'm just killing time while Jane is in class,"

Roxy replied. "So what's a guy like you doing in a booth like this?" She knew it was a cheesy line, but she couldn't resist.

"Fighting for truth, justice, and the American way," he answered. "And cutting loose with some really awesome bands."

Roxy laughed as he launched into a quick dance move. "You're into underground dance music?" she asked.

"Love it. In fact, this club was my idea," he explained. "My goal is to show these guys there's more to today's music than Britney and Justin. There's a whole warehouse band scene just blocks away from our campus. Really fresh stuff. First I want to raise awareness of the club at tomorrow's brunch and with the benefit concert this weekend. Then I want to organize evening music hunts. You know, track undiscovered talent in its natural environment."

"Wow, I'm impressed," Roxy admitted. "You make club-hopping sound like a spiritual quest."

"Hey, it's not just a job, it's an adventure," he said, sliding a clipboard across the counter and handing Roxy a pen. "Sign on the dotted line, please. And don't forget your student ID number."

"But I'm not a student here," Roxy pointed out.

"Sure you are, *Jane*," he insisted. With a foxy grin he picked up her sister's duplicate ID.

Roxy hesitated.

"Oh, come on," he said. "I need the support, and you were just about to do it anyway."

Roxy laughed. "How could I say no to that?" she said. *Oh well. At least it's not belly dancing,* she thought.

Uncapping the pen, she leaned over and signed Rafael's list. "Is that it? Am I a member now?"

"Just one more thing. You need official board approval."

"And how do I get that?" Roxy asked.

"By having lunch with the club president. It's just a formality. Quality control, really."

"Oh, I see," Roxy said, secretly thrilled by Rafael's invitation. Still, she felt like giving him a hard time. "Isn't the club president busy exploring new musical forms? Bravely going where no nightclubber has gone before? And manning the booth in order to find new recruits?"

Rafael shook his head, reaching behind the counter and pulling out a hand-printed sign. "As you can see here, the club president is *Out to Lunch.*"

"Oh, he's out to lunch, all right," she agreed. "Tell me, why should I have lunch with some strange boy?"

"Because I'm *not* some strange boy," he said. "We were introduced . . . by your sister, remember?"

"Oh, I didn't say you were a *stranger*," she replied with a flirty smile. "I said you were *strange.*"

"Well, I can't win that argument," he confessed. "But what do you say? You and me? Food and drink?"

Rafael's gorgeous brown eyes widened to full puppy-dog cuteness.

Roxy considered it. *This guy is definitely trouble*, she thought. *The good kind.*

How could she resist?

8

The Student Union food court was pretty crowded, but Roxy and Rafael managed to find a window seat with a great view of the campus lawn.

Throughout the meal the two compared notes on all their favorite musicians, dividing their likes and dislikes by decade, style, and overall historical importance.

Roxy couldn't believe she'd met someone even more obsessed with music than she was. Rafael really knew his stuff!

"Oh! I almost forgot!" Roxy blurted out, interrupting Rafael in the middle of his extensive analysis of *Billboard*'s current Top Ten. She reached into her backpack and pulled out the flyer Willow had given her. "Check this out. It's an invitation to a party tonight. The Doll Heads are going to play, so the exact location is still a secret. Want to come?"

Rafael's jaw dropped. "A party with the Doll Heads? Are you kidding me? Of course I'll come!"

"Excellent," Roxy said.

"But . . . do you think I can I bring along some members of the Underground Dance Music Club?" he asked. "It sounds like a major must-see."

"Why not?" Roxy said, shrugging. "I'm a friend of the band, after all. And who knows? Maybe I'll jump onstage and shake things up with the ultimate cowbell solo. That ought to bring the house down . . . or the cows home, at least."

Rafael burst out laughing.

I can't believe he's laughing at my corny jokes, Roxy thought. *He may be a keeper.*

Behind her a student screamed—and Roxy jumped. She turned to see a girl laughing and hugging a friend. Roxy sighed and relaxed, relieved it wasn't someone in trouble.

"Boy, you really jumped when that girl screamed," Rafael pointed out. "Is something wrong? You look—I don't know—upset."

I guess that run-in at Penn Station freaked me out more than I thought it did, Roxy realized. She hesitated to tell him about the mugger, but she'd been dying to tell *somebody*. She looked into Rafael's eyes. "Something weird happened yesterday . . . in New York . . . when I went to Penn Station to meet Willow," she began.

Before she knew it, the whole story came flooding out of her: hearing Willow's screams, hitting the mugger with her duffel, being chased through the station, and finally escaping on the train.

"Willow laughed it off. But the more I think about it, the more it bothers me. Why did he try to drag Willow away? Why didn't he just steal her bag? And why did he keep chasing us through the terminal?" Roxy turned and stared out the window. The campus looked so sunny, so peaceful.

Rafael reached across the table and took her hand. "You don't have to worry about that guy anymore. You're here now," he whispered.

Her gaze drifted to the Office of Business Management, where a small group of students spilled out of the doorway and into the sunlight. She thought she saw Jane in the crowd but wasn't sure. She was too far away. But then the blond in the distance pulled out a black leather-bound day planner.

That's Jane, all right, she thought as she watched her sister check off another event in her very busy, very organized schedule.

Then Roxy squinted into the sun, because there—just past Jane—was the man with the mirrored shades.

It can't be, she thought, staring at the man. But it is!

"That's him!" she cried out. "That's the man who chased us!"

Rafael jumped up. "That guy there? Are you sure?"

Now the man was pushing his way through the

crowd, heading toward the Office of Business Management. Toward Jane!

He must think she's me! Roxy realized. "Oh, my God! He's going after my sister. We've got to stop him!"

"Come on!" Rafael shouted, dashing toward the exit.

Roxy grabbed her backpack and followed him.

"There he is!" Rafael said, pointing across the lawn. "You get Jane. Take her into the nearest building and hide. I'll try to block the guy." With that, he spun around and bolted across the lawn.

Roxy turned toward the business building and looked for her sister. She spotted Jane strolling along the pathway with the other students. Jane stopped to jot something in her day planner.

The man in the shades was closing in on her!

Roxy sprinted to the corner of the library. Jane was almost there. She watched the students from Jane's class pass by and waited for her chance.

Then she saw Rafael let out a huge roar and charge straight into the crowd as if he were a soccer player plowing toward the goal line.

A few students jumped out of the way, but the man wasn't so lucky. Rafael smashed right into his stomach, full force, knocking him down to the ground with a heavy thud.

Just a few feet away, Jane turned to see what all

the fuss was about. Roxy reached out, grabbed Jane by the arm, and tugged her into the nearby bushes.

"Hey! Let go!" Jane yelled, smacking away both her sister and the bushes.

"Shut up and follow me," Roxy whispered. "Now!"

She pulled Jane along the bushes in front of the student union and slipped through a side door. "We have to hide," Roxy told her. "Some crazy guy is after us. I'm not kidding around."

Jane looked at Roxy's face. "Okay, I know just the place," she said, grabbing Roxy by the hand and pulling her down a long corridor. They made a right turn, then a left, then another right.

Roxy was getting dizzy. "Are you sure you know where—"

"Yes," Jane whispered. "I know where I'm going." She stopped at a tall door. She opened the door and whispered, "Get in."

Roxy didn't argue. She followed Jane into a huge room that was filled with painted sets, costumes, and trunks full of props. They crouched behind an enormous cardboard tree.

"What is this place?" Roxy asked.

"Shh," Jane hissed. "It's the prop room for the theater. Quiet, someone's coming."

The girls held their breath and listened. Nothing. Then they heard it.

A pair of men's boots clomped heavily on the

THERE'S SOMETHING ABOUT ROXY

floor. Step by step, they seemed to be getting closer.

He must have seen us come in here. He must have got-ten away from Rafael. Please don't find us, she silently begged. *Please*, please *don't find us!*

The footsteps stopped at the door, paused, and then moved on.

Roxy and Jane each let out a sigh of relief.

The footsteps stopped again. Then the girls heard them getting closer and closer.

He's heading straight for us, Roxy thought, her heart pounding.

The boots came to a halt in front of the closed door. The girls didn't dare make a sound.

Roxy watched as the doorknob slowly turned. As the door began to open . . .

9

He found us! Roxy thought, shaking. *It's all over! What is he going to do?*

"Roxy? Jane? Are you guys okay?"

"Rafael!" they both said at once.

Rafael pulled open the door and helped Roxy and Jane out of their hiding place.

"What happened? Are you hurt?" Roxy asked, thinking about his heroic tackle. "And what about that strange man?"

"What strange man?" Jane cut in.

"Once I tackled him, he got up and ran away," Rafael explained. "I chased him off-campus for a few blocks but I lost him."

Jane looked as if she were about to burst. "Will somebody *please* tell me what's going on?" she almost yelled.

"Let's get out of here first and find a place where we can talk," Roxy said.

"How about Campus Security?" Rafael suggested.

• • •

A couple of hours later they sat on the steps in front of the Campus Security office, exhausted by the whole ordeal. Two officers had taken a detailed description of the man and alerted every guard on campus. The chief officer assured them he would report the information to the local police as well.

"Okay, you've told me the whole story, but I still don't get it," Jane said. "Why did he come after *me*?"

"He probably thought you were *me*," Roxy explained.

"So why is he after *you*?" Jane asked.

Rafael offered a theory. "Maybe he figures Roxy knows where Willow is. Think about it. First he grabbed Willow in Penn Station. Then he saw Willow and Roxy take off on a train to Washington. Maybe he somehow knows Willow is in the warehouse district, so he's scanning the whole neighborhood for Willow *and* Roxy. Because if he finds Roxy, he can find out where Willow is hiding."

"What makes you think Willow is hiding?" Roxy asked.

"Well, she's got a box of wigs, doesn't she?" Rafael asked.

Roxy had to admit, Willow was pretty mysterious.

"Okay, okay, your theory makes a lot of sense," Jane agreed. "But tell me this. What does this man want from her? What is Willow hiding?"

Rafael didn't know.

Neither did Roxy. "Good question, Jane," she said. "You can ask her yourself tonight."

"Tonight?" Jane said. "What's tonight?"

"The Underground Dance Music Club is going to see the Doll Heads," Rafael explained.

"So what does that have to do with me?" Jane asked.

Roxy laughed nervously. "Oh, didn't I tell you, Jane?" she said, bracing herself. "I signed you up today. You're their newest member!"

"You did what?" Jane snapped.

"Always glad to help, sis," Roxy said. "You're going to love it."

"That's what you said about your snake," Jane reminded her.

That evening the girls prepared for their night out with the Underground Dance Music Club. Roxy slipped into a black sleeveless club shirt and tight black pants. Then she applied an extra layer of black eyeliner. Jane sighed and slumped back on her bed, not even dressed yet.

"I really, really, *really* hate to ask you this, Roxy," she said. "But do you have anything I could wear?"

Roxy turned away from the mirror, surprised. "What? You're not going to wear your beige sweater set?"

Jane sighed again. "Not tonight. Not for the Doll Heads."

I can't believe it, Roxy thought. *Jane wants to borrow my clothes? If she wasn't being so cool about all my craziness, I'd tease the pants off her.*

"Let's see what I've got," Roxy said, digging into her duffel. She tossed Jane a pink sequined top and a pair of white hip-huggers. "Here. Try these."

Jane started to pull them on but stopped and looked Roxy in the eye. "Can I ask you something?" she said slowly. "Why didn't you tell me about the man with the sunglasses?"

Roxy shrugged. "I didn't want to upset you," she said. Then she confessed her bigger concern. "And I was afraid you'd tell Dad."

Jane looked hurt. "Of course I wouldn't tell Dad," she said. "He would totally freak and make you go home right away. Believe it or not, Roxy, I understand how important this trip is to you. I feel the same way about my school. I wouldn't do anything to jeopardize your Doll Heads education."

Roxy was a little surprised. "Really?" she said. "So we're cool?"

"We're cool," Jane agreed. "But you *are* leaving after the weekend, right?"

Roxy gave her sister a mock punch on the arm just as the dorm-room door burst open with a bang.

It was Jane's roommate, Betsy—the redhead. She

was ready to rock in a black midriff top and a pair of embroidered jeans.

"Hello, ladies!" Betsy said. "Let's party!"

The streetlamps in the warehouse district cast eerie pools of light on the sidewalk, making the tall boy with the shaved head standing at the corner look even more intimidating than he probably was.

Roxy stepped up to the corner, followed by Jane, Rafael, his cousin Claire, Betsy, and a few other students she didn't know. "Let me do the talking," she said softly.

"Don't forget to tell him we're your 'peeps,'" Jane advised.

"Thanks, MC Jane." Roxy marched up to the boy with the shaved head and presented Willow's invitation. "Willow sent us," she said.

The boy gave her a strange look. "Who's Willow?"

That's weird, she thought. *Willow seemed kind of in charge of the whole thing.*

"Well, I'm in with the Doll Heads," Roxy explained. "They're throwing down tonight, right?"

"Chill," the boy replied, doing a quick scan of the streets. "We're trying to keep that 411 on ice."

Roxy nodded as the boy checked out her friends. "You're in," he said. "The icebox is over there. Number nine."

Roxy thanked him and led her group down the

street to a large windowless warehouse. It looked deserted, but when they stepped inside, the whole place throbbed with rhythm and life.

Now this *is what I call a party,* Roxy thought. "Check it out," she said to the others. "Is this cool or what?"

Jane's jaw dropped open. "I have to admit, this is awesome."

The huge silver ballroom glittered with lights and music and energy. Hot-white laser beams darted overhead, mirrored by the pulsing moves of the dancers below. The place was rocking full tilt, and the music was as wild and wonderful as the party-goers themselves.

Betsy was the first of the group to hit the dance floor. Roxy nodded in approval as she started swaying her hips in tune to the pouning beat. Then Rafael's cousin, Claire, jumped in and joined her. Back at the school Claire had seemed so reserved, but now, with hair gel and a black leather jacket, she looked like a punked-out rock star. Roxy bobbed her head and watched as a few other students hopped into the mix.

"Feel like dancing with a *strange* boy?" Rafael whispered into her ear.

Roxy smiled and pretended to look around. "Which one?" she asked.

"This one," he answered. With that, he spun her onto the dance floor, and the music swept the two of them away.

Rafael was a great dancer—and it was a great opportunity for Roxy to check him out in his black T-shirt and jeans. She hadn't realized before what big shoulders and arms he had. She could barely keep herself from staring.

Her view was suddenly blocked by a blur of red hair. Betsy bounced in front of her and blurted out, "Check out the cute boy trying to get Jane to dance with him."

Roxy turned and looked. Jane stood on the edge of the dance floor with her arms folded across her chest. Bobbing side to side in front of her was an adorable punk boy with spiky blond hair, a ripped black T-shirt, and studded pants. He pointed at the dance floor, then at Jane and himself, and offered his hand.

Jane smiled and shrugged. To Roxy's amazement, she accepted the boy's offer. "Go for it, Jane!" Roxy shouted.

They watched as Jane stepped onto the dance floor, one inch at a time, as if she were easing into a swimming pool filled with cold water. The punk boy was way ahead of her, swiveling his hips and waving his arms like a madman. Jane made a half hearted attempt to get into the groove.

"Come on, Jane!" Roxy shouted again. "Go for it!"

Jane ignored her sister and, after a few awkward moves, started rocking to the beat. Roxy couldn't believe her eyes. Jane was really letting go. Her whole body loosened up, and she started to move to the music. She even tossed her head until her hair whipped across her face.

"You shake it, girl!" Roxy cheered proudly as she bounced to the beat herself.

Suddenly the music changed, and the pulsing beat melted away into a slow, silky smooth mix of hip-hop and soul.

Rafael took Roxy's hand and pulled her into his arms. "This is nice," he said sweetly.

"Yes, it is," she agreed. *It's more than nice*, she thought as they swayed to the beat. She looked up into his beautiful brown eyes. "I never really thanked you for what you did today, Rafael. Man, you really tackled that guy. I'm impressed."

"Hey, what are friends for?" he said, his voice soft and low.

"Just friends?" Roxy asked coyly.

Rafael smiled and drew her even closer, his lips about to touch hers.

Roxy closed her eyes, ready for the moment.

But then the music ended. Someone stepped onto the stage next to the dance floor, and all the guests burst into applause.

"I'd like to thank you all for coming to my party."

Roxy pulled away from Rafael and focused her attention on the stage. "That's her! That's Willow!" she said.

Rafael turned around to get a look as Willow crossed the stage with a microphone.

Willow's hair was beautifully styled—no wig this time—and her dress was by a top designer. She blew a few kisses to the crowd, and everyone cheered. Then, when the applause died down, she started to speak again.

"On TV they have programs they like to call 'very special episodes.' Problem is, they're never very special."

The audience chuckled.

"This, however, is a very special party. And to prove just how special it is, I'd like to introduce my friends . . . the Doll Heads!"

The place went crazy. Everybody clapped, hooted and whistled as Johnny Whisper and the rest of the band stepped onto the stage. Willow gave Johnny a quick peck on the cheek and sauntered off. The concert began.

The Doll Heads ripped into their first song with a hard throbbing beat and an explosion of guitars. The crowd cheered when they recognized the band's biggest hit, which sounded even more incredible being played live.

This is so awesome! Roxy thought, grooving a little with the crowd. *But I've got to talk to Willow. I've got to tell her I saw the guy from Penn Station again.*

Rafael started to dance again, but Roxy grabbed

him by one arm and pulled him toward the stage. "Let's find Willow. She's got some explaining to do." Weaving through the crowd, Roxy pointed across the dance floor. "There she is."

Willow was dancing wildly next to the stage with two other girls.

Rafael moved in closer for a better look. "I swear I've seen her somewhere before," he said staring at her. "She looks so familiar, but I can't place her. Who is she?"

At that moment Willow spotted Roxy and waved. Roxy started to wave back. Then Willow's expression changed.

What's the matter with her? Roxy thought.

Willow quickly spun around and hurried to an exit door.

"Wait! Willow!" Roxy cried. Why was she running away?

"I guess she won't be answering any questions tonight," Rafael pointed out.

"We'll see." Roxy grabbed Rafael's hand and dashed after her friend, following her out the door and into the street.

But they were too late. Willow was climbing into a cab, and before they could stop her, she slammed the door and took off.

That's so strange, Roxy thought.

Stranger still, Roxy saw the man with the shades

standing at the curb, trying to catch his breath. He had missed the cab by just a few seconds.

And strangest of all, Roxy saw Willow roll down the window of the cab and blow a kiss to the man who had been chasing her!

10

Roxy snuck out of the dorm early the next morning, tiptoeing past Jane, who wore an eye mask and slept like a log, and her roommate, Betsy, who snored.

She rushed through the lobby, giving the receptionist a fast, friendly wave.

"Good morning," the gray-haired woman replied with a wink.

Roxy winked back without even thinking.

Stepping out into the warm morning light, she crossed the campus and headed straight for the warehouse district. It was time to find out what was up with Willow, once and for all.

But when she reached Scratch's warehouse, nobody seemed to be home—or awake. She pressed the buzzer a second time, then a third, and waited. Nothing.

Finally giving up, Roxy had no choice but to head back to the school. She looked over at the factory next door. *The Doll Heads are probably asleep too*, she thought, *especially after last night's performance. It went pretty late. Still, it can't hurt to try.* She marched up to the door and pushed the buzzer.

After a minute or two Johnny swung open the door. "Roxy! Good morning! Come on in!" He hustled Roxy inside and led her to the rehearsal hall.

Sneaky Pete, Jones, and Face seemed happy to see her, too.

"Me and the boys are trying a different approach to our new song," Johnny explained. "What do you think?"

Roxy was thrilled to get to listen to the Doll Heads play again. But then she remembered why she'd come here in the first place. "Sure, Johnny. I'd love to hear it," she said. "But first, I want to ask you something. Do you know where Willow is?"

Johnny wrinkled his nose. "Who?"

Is he kidding? Roxy wondered.

At that moment the back door opened and in walked Willow—looking as mysterious as ever in a short red wig. "Morning, guys," she cooed. "Another drop-dead performance last night. Thanks a million." Then she noticed Roxy in the corner. "Oh, hi, Rox. Did you have fun last night?"

"Yes, thanks," she answered. "Until you ran away."

The smile faded from Willow's face. Taking a deep breath, she sat down next to Roxy while the band tuned their instruments. "Look, Rox," she began, "I didn't want to scare you, but I saw that creep from Penn Station last night at the party. I just panicked and took off. I'm sorry. I should have warned you."

"But who is he? Why did he follow you here?" Roxy asked.

Willow shook her head. "I don't know. Maybe he thinks I'm somebody else."

Roxy wasn't satisfied with her answer. "He went after my sister yesterday. Then he ran after your cab last night. He obviously wants something, and he's not giving up. Whoever he is, he has to be stopped. And I could swear I saw you blow him a kiss."

Willow put a hand on Roxy's shoulder. "A kiss? No way! Just the opposite. Last night I took that cab straight to the police. I heard they arrested him in Virginia. He's just some weirdo."

"Really?" Roxy said, surprised and relieved. "That's good. But there's still something else I need to know."

"Shoot," Willow said.

Roxy hesitated before asking. "Who are you, Willow? Really."

"Well, I—" Willow began.

"Roxy! Get over here! Do you remember what we did yesterday with the cymbal? Could you do it again for me?" Johnny shouted across the room.

"For real?" Roxy asked. She looked at Willow.

"Hold that thought. I'll be right back." She scrambled to her feet, grabbed the cymbal, and took her place next to Johnny. Out of the corner of her eye she saw Willow wave and slip out the back door.

"Willow! Let's talk later!" Roxy shouted after her. But Willow was gone.

"Okay, Roxy. Let me have it," Johnny said.

Roxy grabbed her cymbal and drumstick and nodded. She knew she'd have another chance to talk to Willow. Who knew when she'd have another chance to rock? "One! Two! Three! Four!"

"Where have you been?" Jane demanded when Roxy returned to the dorm later that morning.

"With the Doll Heads," she answered, her mind still swimming from the jam session. She leaned in the doorway. "What a blast."

"Well, the brunch is just an hour away," Jane went on, pacing the dorm room. "Remember the brunch? Remember your boyfriend, Rafael?"

"He's not my boyfriend." Roxy smiled. "Not yet."

"Well, he won't be if you blow off this brunch. The benefit concert is very important to Rafael. And me."

"I know." Roxy flopped down onto the bed, and Jane nearly had a heart attack.

"Watch it! You're going to wrinkle the skirt and blazer I picked out for you!"

Roxy groaned. "Me? In a skirt and blazer?"

"Why not? You dressed me up last night," Jane shot back. "Now it's my turn. Hurry up. Get changed."

"Chill out, Jane. We have plenty of time." Roxy jumped up from the bed.

"I will not chill out, and we do not have plenty of time. We have a million things to go over. We do not want to make fools of ourselves."

"Don't worry, I won't pick up my food with my toes or anything," Roxy said.

"This brunch is a big deal," Jane went on. "We need people to sponsor the benefit concert to raise money for the school. Rafael's parents have invited politicians, business owners, local celebrities, and even some people from the *Washington Post*. You don't want to embarrass yourself in front of Rafael and the *Washington Post*, do you?"

"No," Roxy grumbled.

"Okay, then," Jane teased. "A waiter brings you a bowl of soup. Which spoon do you use?"

"The one without the holes," Roxy joked. "Don't worry, Jane. I'll behave."

Roxy did as she was told and started to get dressed in the clothes that Jane picked out for her.

Jane fastened another button on the white blouse she'd lent her, then tied a light ruffled scarf around her neck. To finish it all off, she made Roxy try on a pale gray blazer.

"There you go," Jane said, pushing Roxy in front

of the full-length mirror hanging on the door. "See how professional you look?"

Roxy studied her reflection. "I look like you, Jane."

"I'll take that as a compliment."

"But I'm *not* you. I'm *me*, and I'm suffocating." Roxy reached up and tugged at the scarf.

Jane gasped. "Stop that! You'll ruin the bow!"

"It's summer, Jane. It's hot."

"It's stylish, Roxy. It's summer-weight fabric. Deal with it." Jane turned and picked up her purse, double-checking to make sure she had everything, including her day planner, antibacterial hand wipes, breath mints, and personal contact cards.

"Okay, I'm all set. You pull yourself together, and I'll meet you with the others in front of the library in eight minutes." She started to go.

Roxy's stomach flipped. *I'm a nervous wreck*, she realized.

"Jane?" she said.

Jane stopped in the doorway. "Yes?"

"Can I tell you something?" Roxy asked in a soft voice.

Jane turned around. "Tell me what?"

"I'm nervous," Roxy admitted.

Jane smiled. "Nervous? You? I don't believe it."

Roxy nodded. "A little," she admitted. "I-I didn't realize this was going to be some sort of grand event.

And it's *so* not my thing. Between all those hotshots coming to the brunch and all that stuff you know . . . I just hope I can pull it off."

Jane sighed. "Roxy, you're smart, funny, and talented. And you know which soup spoon to use. Everyone's going to love you. They always do." She paused and smiled. "There's something about you, Roxy. And this time I mean it as a compliment."

Roxy broke out into a huge grin. "Thanks, Jane. Thanks for everything."

Jane left the room, and Roxy was alone.

She stared at her reflection in the mirror. *I guess this outfit is pretty. . . .* she thought. *But it's just not me.*

Roxy appreciated everything her sister was trying to do for her, but it didn't help. The girl in the mirror was *not* Roxy Ryan. Not at all.

Roxy glanced around the room, unsure what to do, when her gaze fell upon a black T-shirt on the floor. Then she figured it out. *Sorry, Jane,* she thought, tearing off the ruffled scarf.

11

"Only you, Roxy," Jane mumbled as they approached Rafael's house. "Only you would wear a David Bowie T-shirt with a skirt and blazer set."

"I thought a black shirt would look nice with the pale gray," Roxy pointed out. "And *it's* summer-weight, too."

Jane didn't laugh.

At least she's talking to me again, Roxy thought. *I still can't believe she stewed over the shirt for the whole train ride to Georgetown. Good thing Betsy and Claire came with us.*

"This is the place," Claire said.

The girls stopped in front an elegant brownstone. Dark green ivy covered the sides of the house, and, even though it was lunchtime, a pair of gaslight lamps flickered on either side of the door.

Wow, Roxy thought. *Nice digs.*

Betsy rapped twice with the antique knocker. Roxy noticed Betsy wasn't wearing a midriff top anymore. Today she was dressed in a mint-green suit.

I wonder if Jane dressed her, too, Roxy thought with a slight smile.

The door swung open, and a tall bald man in a black suit greeted the girls.

Talk about formal, Roxy thought, suddenly nervous again. *Oh, well. Just relax and be friendly.* "Hello, Mr. Delfino," she said, holding out her right hand. "I'm your son's friend, Roxy."

"How do you do, miss?" he said, not taking her hand. "I'm afraid I'm not Mr. Delfino. I'm his butler. Won't you please come with me?"

Roxy blushed. *Go with it*, she told herself, trying not to feel like a complete idiot. "Uh, sure," she said.

The girls followed the butler through the main hallway of the house. Roxy was stunned by how beautiful it was, with its checkered marble floors and rich wood paneling. But what really got her was the artwork—the place was practically a museum, full of paintings and sculptures.

"Man! Does someone really live here?" she couldn't help blurting out.

Jane elbowed her in the ribs.

"Hey!" Rafael came bounding down the hall, looking outrageously handsome in a cream jacket and black tie.

Maybe I should have worn the blouse, Roxy thought.

"You guys made it," Rafael greeted them all.

"Let's go out to the courtyard. Since it's such a nice day, my mom decided to have the brunch outside by the waterfall."

"Waterfall?" Roxy asked, still shocked by the splendor of her surroundings. "You have a waterfall?"

"Yeah, it's a pool really, but my dad likes the sound of falling water. . . ."

"Who doesn't?" Roxy said with a grin.

Rafael led the girls through a dazzling conservatory filled with sunlight and exotic plants. The double doors at the far end opened up to a courtyard, and Roxy could see the other guests mingling by the waterfall and pool.

The buffet of food was arranged on a long table at one end of the pool. At the other end water tumbled over a rocky ledge into the pool.

Betsy and Claire headed straight for the food while Jane checked out the crowd and pulled out her day planner.

"Let's see. A couple of senators, a few stockbrokers, a Fortune 500 businessman or two," Jane muttered under her breath. She jotted down a few notes, then said, "It's showtime." With that, she trotted off to drum up donations.

Roxy had to admire her sister's determination. She herself didn't have a clue how to approach these people.

"Come meet my parents," Rafael whispered into Roxy's ear. "They're going to love you."

Okay, now I'm officially terrified, she thought.

Rafael took her hand and led her across the courtyard. They approached a beautifully dressed couple, who was chatting with a tall older man with white hair.

"Sorry to interrupt," Rafael said, "but I'd like to introduce you to someone." He put his arm around Roxy's waist. "Mom, Dad, this is Roxanne Ryan, the girl I was telling you about."

Rafael's mom looks like a movie star, Roxy thought. *Tall, tanned, and totally gorgeous.*

"Hi, Roxy," the woman greeted her warmly. "Rafael has told us so many fascinating things about you."

"I'll admit to nothing without my lawyer," Roxy said, hoping his mom would think that was funny.

Rafael's mother laughed and flashed a dazzling grin.

Now I know where Rafael gets his smile, she thought. *And I bet he got those amazing brown eyes from his father.* Roxy looked up to see if her guess was right, but Rafael's father was staring at her T-shirt.

"Is that a David Bowie T-shirt you're wearing?" he asked.

Uh-oh, Roxy thought, glancing down at her top, *big mistake*.

"I love it!" Rafael's father exclaimed. "I saw Bowie in London before he hit it big. Those were the days." He turned to introduce the white-haired man beside him. "Roxy, meet Senator Darling. He was just telling me that people don't remember the past and then you show up wearing a David Bowie T-shirt. It proves that some things, like a great rock star, never get old."

"Nice to meet you, Roxy," said the senator.

Roxy smiled. Feeling more comfortable, she decided it was safe to turn on the charm. "The pleasure's mine, darling," she replied. "I mean, Senator Darling."

Roxy was relieved when everybody laughed.

"I wore this shirt to remind everyone what this brunch is for," she explained. "Besides raising money for the John Adams School, the Music Club's benefit concert is a great opportunity to expose people to all kinds of music—old and new. We're trying to line up a couple of really cool new bands from the warehouse district."

"Really? My son moved into one of those warehouses," said the senator. "He's trying to become a sound mixer, and he's looking for a band to produce. He calls himself Scratch."

"I know Scratch!" Roxy burst out. "He's your son? Wow. Scratch is a great guy. He's got a killer collection of concert posters."

"And a little mouse problem," the senator added.

The two of them burst out laughing.

Ten minutes later Roxy had Senator Darling pledging a large donation for the concert.

• • •

The brunch was in full swing now, and Roxy was thrilled with the results. She met up with Jane, who had just gotten a young businesswoman to make a donation.

"I can't believe how many donations you got. You're really kicking butt!" Roxy said.

Jane shrugged. "Thanks. You're not doing so badly yourself."

Rafael came up behind them. "*Both* of you are cleaning up here," he told them. "Between the two of you we've raised enough money to pay for all the sound and light equipment, plus security and clean-up crews."

Jane pulled out her day planner and flipped it open to her checklist. "We're right on schedule. Keep up the good work." She slapped her book shut and was off to get more donations.

Then Rafael pulled Roxy away and introduced her to one of Washington's most successful real estate developers.

"So where are you planning to have this concert?" the businessman asked.

Rafael stepped into the conversation. "The school athletic complex," he answered.

Roxy made a face. "Too bad it can't be outside," she said. "The weather's been so beautiful."

"Of course it should be outside! It's summer!" the businessman agreed. "And I know just the place. I own some land along the Potomac. It's right near the school. It would be perfect!"

Moments later Rafael and the real estate man were shaking hands and exchanging phone numbers.

"You're amazing," Rafael whispered to Roxy. "You just scored the best location in the city."

Roxy couldn't stop smiling—until she saw Rafael's mother rushing toward them with a pained look on her face. "We've got a problem," she informed them. "I promised musical entertainment at this brunch—the Canticle String Quartet, in fact—but their van broke down in Maryland. Only the cellist made it. Poor man, look at him playing by himself."

Rafael and Roxy heard the deep, somber strains of the cello. It sounded pretty lonely and sad, casting a sense of doom and gloom over the whole party.

"Look. Some of the guests are starting to leave," Rafael's mother went on. "This is a disaster. The man from the *Washington Post* just showed up, and it looks like the party is over. We have to find a way to keep people here a little longer."

Roxy tried to think fast. Reaching into a pocket, she pulled out her cell phone. "The party's not over yet," she said. "I know someone who can help."

She speed-dialed Johnny Whisper.

12

"Thanks for doing this, Johnny," Roxy said when he arrived at the party thirty minutes later.

Johnny shrugged. "I figure, why not? It gives me a chance to show off my classical training. I like to surprise people."

Roxy received a surprise of her own when Rafael walked out of the house lugging a huge upright bass. He set the bulky instrument down behind Johnny Whisper and the cello player and started tuning the strings.

"I didn't know you played the bass," Roxy said, truly impressed.

Rafael blushed. "It's not something I advertise. I was teased about it a lot as a kid."

As the makeshift trio of musicians prepared to play, Roxy and Jane gathered the guests around to make an announcement.

"Ladies and gentlemen," Jane started off, "we'd like to thank you for attending today's brunch. Your generous donations will help support new programs and scholarships for the John Adams School. Thanks to you, our Music Club's benefit concert on Saturday is sure to be a great success."

Roxy took it from there. "Now let's get this show on the road. We have a special surprise for you today, a rare classical performance from a legend of rock and roll. Ladies and gentlemen . . . Johnny Whisper of the Doll Heads!"

The guests applauded politely, not sure what to expect. The courtyard grew silent.

Raising the bow to his violin, Johnny launched into a Mozart sonata with the same raw energy he brought to his greatest rock hits. The effect was electrifying. Rafael and the cellist joined in with a more traditional approach to the music. Roxy found the blend of modern and classical absolutely mesmerizing.

And so did the guests. When the trio finished their first piece, the crowd erupted with hearty applause and bravos.

"Looks like you've done it again, Roxy," Jane whispered as the performance continued.

"I didn't do it alone, Jane. Look at how much money you raised. And look at Rafael. He's really talented."

"Yeah," Jane agreed. "He's a keeper, Rox."

At that moment Rafael looked up from his bass and, spotting the sisters, burst into a huge grin.

Roxy smiled through the rest of the performance.

When it was all over, the reporter from the *Washington Post* asked to take pictures of Johnny Whisper and the other musicians. He even made Jane and Roxy pose in a few shots.

"Where did you learn to play like that, Mr. Whisper?" the newsman asked.

"I studied classical music at the John Adams School," Johnny answered to everyone's surprise.

"Oh, I see," the newsman responded. "Will you be appearing at the school's benefit concert this Saturday?"

Johnny flashed Roxy a smile. "I'd do anything to help my friends."

"Get up. Get up, Roxy." Jane shook her awake.

Roxy rolled over in the sleeping bag on the floor and opened her eyes. The girl who was staring down at her *sounded* like her sister, but she didn't *look* like her sister.

Jane's hair was teased out and her usual wardrobe was replaced by a ripped denim skirt, black stockings, high-heeled boots, and a fitted basketball jersey.

"Please tell me I'm still sleeping," Roxy groaned. "What's the story, Jane?"

"*This* is the story," Jane answered, tossing a copy of the *Washington Post* onto the bed. "Page one of today's Style section. And I quote, 'The legendary

Doll Heads have agreed to play at the John Adams School benefit concert this Saturday.'"

Roxy sat up and snatched the paper. Her eyes were immediately drawn to a large photograph of Johnny Whisper and his violin, posed between Jane and herself.

"This is awesome!" Roxy squealed. "Everybody will want to come to the concert now!"

"I know. That's the problem," Jane groaned, flopping onto the floor beside her.

"That's not a problem, Jane. The fact that my eyes are closed in the picture—now *that's* a problem."

"Don't you see? The newspaper got it wrong. Johnny didn't guarantee the band would play. He said he needed to talk to them first."

Roxy wasn't too worried. "I'm sure they'll do it if Johnny asks them."

"But what if they won't?" Jane asked.

Roxy shrugged. "They will. Johnny's a graduate of the school. He said he'd help out any way he could."

Jane stood up and crossed the room. "Well, I don't think we should take any chances. We need to talk to Johnny and the band. We need to book the Doll Heads—*now*."

"Well, that explains the rock-and-roll-diva duds," Roxy muttered.

"Just get dressed. And no wisecracks about my clothes," Jane warned, primping before the mirror.

"Okay, Madonna," Roxy said, getting up to shower. Before she knew it, she and Jane were hurrying through the lobby as fast as they could. Roxy and Jane gave their usual little wave to the winking receptionist. But this time Jane winked back at her.

"Don't do that, Jane!" Roxy scolded playfully. "She's going to think you're making fun of her."

"I forgot." Jane groaned. "Maybe she'll just think I like her."

Roxy laughed and followed her sister out the door, where they both nearly collided with Rafael.

"I was just coming to see you guys," he said, a little out of breath. "We need to talk."

"Did you see the *Post*?" Jane asked.

Rafael nodded. "My phone hasn't stopped ringing since this morning, and my e-mail is totally flooded. Right now there's a mob forming at the Student Union building. Everybody wants tickets!"

"We're going to talk to Johnny right now," Jane said.

"We *have* to book the Doll Heads," Rafael stressed, "or else we'll have a very angry audience Saturday night."

"Okay! Okay! I'm on the case!" Roxy assured him. "Come on, Jane. Let's go."

They started to dash off, but Rafael stopped them. "Wait! I just had to tell you, Roxy. My parents loved you. They were very impressed."

Roxy blushed. "Well, I'm impressed that your dad saw Bowie in London. And your mom was so nice. No wonder you turned out so cool."

"Really?" Rafael smiled.

And Jane yanked Roxy's arm. "No time for flirting, Roxy. Come on."

The two headed off across the campus and were passing the library when a cute blond preppy boy came running after them. "Hey, Jane! Wait up!"

"Who's he?" Roxy asked.

Jane shrugged. "Don't know."

"It's me, Jason," he said. "We danced at the party, remember?"

Roxy saw it now. It was the adorable punk boy from the night before! But now, instead of a ripped T-shirt and studded pants, he wore a short-sleeved Oxford shirt under a pale blue sweater vest with a pair of khakis. And his spiky hair was soft and combed down.

"Are you in the summer program here?" Jane asked.

"Yeah, believe it or not," he answered with a boyish grin. "I'm an economics major."

"Really?" Jane said, batting her eyes. "Maybe we have a class together."

Roxy leaned over and whispered into her ear. "No time for flirting, Jane. *Remember?*"

Jane shot her sister a dirty look, then wrapped up her conversation with Jason. They didn't waste any more time getting off campus, heading straight for the Doll Heads' factory without stopping.

"This is it?" Jane asked, staring at the old brick building. "It doesn't look very glamorous . . . or very clean." She pulled out her packet of hand wipes.

"I guess you could call it grunge glam," Roxy said, pressing the buzzer. "Wait until you see the rehearsal hall." She buzzed again.

Finally someone shouted from inside the building. "Come in! It's unlocked!"

Roxy pushed open the door and led Jane back to the huge rehearsal hall with hundreds of doll heads hanging from the ceiling.

Johnny Whisper sat alone, cross-legged on the floor in the middle of the room. He was slumped over the *Washington Post*.

This doesn't look good, Roxy thought. "Um, hi, Johnny," she said nervously. "Did you, um, happen to read the Style section of the *Post*?"

Johnny nodded slowly but didn't say anything.

Oh, no. He's ticked off, Roxy thought. "I have to apologize about that," she tried to explain. "I guess the reporter misunderstood. I guess he assumed the Doll Heads would play at the concert, since you're a graduate of the school. You *did* say you'd do anything to help out, right?"

Johnny looked up at them. "I would," he said. "I'd be happy to play."

Jane and Roxy started to smile.

"But there's one problem," Johnny went on.

The smiles faded. "A problem?" Roxy asked.

Johnny nodded and sighed. "The Doll Heads are splitting up."

13

Roxy and Jane were completely speechless.

How could the Doll Heads split up? They were one of the hottest bands to hit the music scene in years!

"You know how we've been having some trouble—creative differences," Johnny started to explain.

Roxy remembered the recording session the band had canceled back in New York—and the angry producer.

"I want to do something new," Johnny went on. "I want to capture the echo of music in raw spaces, not in a slick studio. I want to blend rock and soul and classical but keep it simple and real."

"But that's what you guys were doing," Roxy told him. "Those jam sessions sounded great."

"I thought so, too," Johnny admitted, "but the rest of the band isn't sure. They went home to their families for a few days to decide if we should keep trying . . . or quit."

"You can't quit! You're Johnny Whisper! You're the Doll Heads!" Roxy protested.

Johnny shrugged. "But I kind of feel like a scratched-up CD, playing the same old song over and over."

Roxy shook her head. "That's ridiculous. Your performance at the brunch yesterday was genius. The way you played violin as if it were an electric guitar . . . I've never heard anything like it. You're one of a kind, Johnny."

Johnny almost cracked a smile. "Thanks, Roxy. Maybe you're right. Maybe I should try going solo."

That wasn't what Roxy had meant, but it gave her an idea. "Maybe you *should* try going solo," she said. "You can test it out tomorrow night at the concert for the school."

Johnny's eyes widened. "That's a brilliant idea, Roxy! I can try out all my new songs!"

Roxy glanced at her sister.

Jane had been holding her breath through the whole discussion, and now she let it out. "That's great! Yes!"

"But wait. No," Johnny said, frowning. "I can't perform alone. I need a backup band. I need an engineer to mix the sound."

"I can pound the piano for you, Johnny." Willow's voice echoed from the back of the room. Wearing a long black wig and a short dress, she strolled through the back doorway of the factory and struck a pose.

Scratch sauntered in behind her. "I can do the sound mix," he volunteered.

"Really? That would be so amazing. Thanks, guys." Johnny's face seemed to light up. He looked back at all the instruments behind him, and Roxy could tell his mind was racing with possibilities. He turned back and looked at her. "Your friend Rafael is a terrific bass player," he said. "Do you think he'd play with me at the concert?"

Oh, please, Roxy thought. *Rafael is still bouncing off the walls from the brunch performance yesterday. He'll be totally psyched.* "I'll twist his arm," she told Johnny, smiling.

Johnny clapped and spun around to a pile of rumpled sheet music and started taking notes. He asked Scratch to look over some ideas he had for the sound design.

"I have to get to a lecture," Jane said, glancing at her watch. "Rafael will be there. Is it okay if I tell him the news?"

Roxy said sure and waved good-bye. Then she turned to Willow. "I didn't know you played the piano," Roxy said.

Willow shrugged. "I can plunk out a tune."

"You know, that reminds me. You never answered my question yesterday." Roxy looked her straight in the eye. "Who are you? Really."

Willow took a deep breath and sat on a stool. "Roxy, have you ever been treated a certain way simply because of how you look or how you dress or how you do something? Some people will just stick you into a box and say 'she's this' or 'she's that' and never even try to get to know you."

Roxy nodded. She could totally relate to that.

Willow went on. "Sometimes I like to bust out of that box. I just toss on a wig and invent a new name, and I can be whatever I want. I don't have to be 'this' or 'that.' I can be me."

Roxy was still dying to know the truth, but she respected Willow's wish to escape whatever box people had put her in. "That's cool, Willow," she said.

Both of them smiled. Johnny and Scratch came over and asked Willow if she had one of the band's rehearsal tapes back at the loft. The three of them decided to go hunt for it, asking Roxy if she minded waiting. As they walked out the back door, the last thing she heard was Johnny say, "Now all we need is a drummer."

The door closed, and Roxy was alone in the huge rehearsal hall. She slowly wandered around, examining all the guitars and basses. Some were electric, others acoustic—all cool. She moved on. And stopped at the drum set.

If you can dream it, you can do it, Roxy, she reminded herself. *Don't give up.* She imagined herself onstage, banging out a beat with Johnny, Rafael, and Willow at the benefit concert on Saturday. . . .

That gave her an idea.

Her fingers instinctively picked up a pair of the drumsticks. Twirling one, then the other, she brought the sticks down hard on the snare. Before she knew it, she was pounding out a beat, getting bolder with every stroke.

Hey, not bad, she thought. Picking up the tempo, she launched into a double combination, then a triple, and ended it all with a shimmering cymbal clash.

Closing her eyes, Roxy basked in the imaginary sound of applause—and almost fell off her stool when she realized the sound was real. She opened her eyes.

Johnny Whisper stood in the doorway . . . and he was clapping! "I think I've found my drummer," he said.

After hours and hours of rehearsal with Johnny Roxy and Rafael were exhausted—and exhilarated— as they strolled arm in arm back to the school.

"It's going to be great," Rafael gushed. "I can't believe how awesome we sound together."

"You and Johnny sound awesome," Roxy agreed. "I'm not so sure about my drumming. Good thing Johnny threw blankets over the drums to muffle the sound."

Rafael rolled his eyes. "That's just so you won't drown out the acoustic instruments. You sound amazing. I think you've really found the key to the music."

"Thanks. That means a lot to me," Roxy said. "By the way, what do you think happened to Willow? She said she had to go take care of something, but she didn't come back. She missed the whole rehearsal."

"I don't know. Johnny told me that she needed to disappear but that she'd be back in time for the concert."

"Well, I hope she's telling the truth about being able to play the piano," Roxy said, a little worried.

"Hey! Look!" Rafael interrupted by pointing out the new concert posters plastered across the campus. "I see Claire and Betsy have been doing their jobs."

"You bet your bass we have," Betsy said, jumping out from behind a library column with a roll of tape in her hand and Claire by her side.

"We're totally beat," Claire gasped, waving a stack of posters and a schedule book. "Ever since the brunch, Jane, Betsy, and I have been making phone calls, moving the location to the riverside lot, renting the stage equipment, hiring security guards . . . but enough about us. How's the band?"

Rafael and Roxy gave them a quick update, then they all decided to rest up for the big day. It was already after midnight.

When they reached the girls' dorm, Roxy glanced at Rafael and suddenly wished they hadn't run into Betsy and Claire. *I'm leaving on Sunday*, she realized with a start, *and Rafael and I haven't even kissed.*

But they weren't alone, and instead of a soft kiss on the lips, Rafael left her with a friendly wave. "See you guys tomorrow," he said.

Once inside the dorm, Claire headed straight for her room, while Roxy and Betsy slipped quietly into their room. They tiptoed in, just in case Jane was asleep.

"Hey, guys," Jane said, glancing up from a huge history textbook propped up on her lap. "How are things in the exciting world of rock and roll? Making history as we speak?"

Roxy laughed and told Jane all the details about the rehearsal while Betsy changed into a flannel nightgown dotted with clouds and sheep. Jane, like Roxy, seemed a little worried about Willow's latest disappearance.

"What if she's a no-show?" Jane asked.

"I don't know." Roxy shook her head. She did not want to imagine that possibility.

She slipped into a nightshirt, grabbed a pillow, and unrolled the sleeping bag on the floor. Jane closed her history book, and Betsy snapped out the light.

Staring into the darkness, Roxy couldn't sleep.

"Jane? You still awake?" she whispered.

"Yes. What?"

"I'm so nervous about tomorrow night, I could scream."

"Please don't," Jane said.

"Can I really get up there and play drums in front of all those people?" Roxy wondered aloud.

"Come on, Roxy. From what I've seen, you can do anything you put your mind to," Jane said. "You always land on your feet."

Roxy had to smile. "Gee, thanks, Jane. If it wasn't for you and the John Adams School, I'd never have this chance."

The girls giggled softly in the darkness.

"Okay, Oprah and Dr. Phil," Betsy blurted out. "Shut up. I need my beauty sleep."

When everyone finally stopped laughing, Roxy closed her eyes and tried to sleep.

I can't sleep, she realized. *What if today was just a fluke and I stink tomorrow? I'll embarrass Rafael and Jane, and they've both worked so hard on this concert. Worst of all, I'll embarrass Johnny Whisper.*

Roxy tried to push the thought out of her mind. She remembered what her dad always told her to do when she was upset. *Just relax and get a good night's sleep.*

She was almost dozing off when Jane whispered something to her. "Not to put any more pressure on you, Roxy, but I talked to Dad again today."

"Really?" Roxy answered groggily.

"Yeah," Jane said. "He's coming to the concert tomorrow."

Roxy gulped. *So much for a good night's sleep.*

14

The big night arrived—and Roxy's nerves were shot.

The stage was in place, the speakers and lights were up, and the riverside lot was jam-packed with eager fans.

Roxy tried to calm herself by staring out at the Potomac River. The rippling water reflected the last rays of sunlight, and soon Roxy felt her stage fright drifting away. It was going to be a perfect summer night.

Just calm down, she told herself. *Everything's going to be okay*. You're *going to be okay*. It felt weird giving *herself* the pep talk. Jane was usually the stressed-out basket case.

"Roxy, Willow's not here yet," Jane said, grabbing her by the arm and shaking it. "What are we going to do? What are we going to *do*?"

Roxy's stomach flipped. She spun around and saw Rafael, Scratch, and Johnny by the side of the stage. "What should we do?" she asked them.

"We can't wait much longer," Rafael explained. "Everything's ready—the instruments, the microphones, the sound check—and the audience is getting restless."

Johnny made a fast decision. "We go on without her," he said. "Everybody, take your places. And, Roxy? Break a leg."

Break a leg? Roxy thought. *Are you kidding? I can barely walk, I'm so nervous. I've never performed onstage before.* Taking a deep breath, she turned to the stage—and almost crashed into a petite young blond.

It was Willow!

"Ready to rock?" Willow asked with a wink.

Roxy hardly recognized her in the new platinum wig and white lace dress. "Willow! You made it! I was worried about you!"

"Of *course* I made it," she said, waving them up the stairs to the stage. "Let's do this."

Willow, Roxy, and Rafael walked out onto the stage, sparking an explosion of cheers from the crowd. Roxy took her place behind an assortment of drums wrapped in blankets. Rafael picked up his large wooden bass. Willow waltzed over to a baby grand piano and, seating herself gracefully, tore off her wig.

Some people whistled and cheered, then the audience quieted down and waited.

Soon Scratch's voice echoed from the speakers.

"Ladies and gentlemen, the John Adams School is proud to present . . . Johnny Whisper and the Three Blind Mice."

Roxy, Rafael, and Willow slipped on dark sunglasses and smiled. Then Johnny bounded onto the stage with his violin and the crowd went crazy.

Roxy's heart was pounding. She scanned the crowd and spotted all the people she knew—Betsy, Claire, Rafael's parents, Senator Darling, Jason the preppy punk, even the winking receptionist! Then she saw Jane standing next to their father. They both looked so proud.

Roxy glanced back at Johnny, who gave her the thumbs-up. *This is it*, she told herself. Then she took a deep breath—and kicked off the concert with the click of her drumsticks. "One! Two! Three! Four!"

Roxy laid down the beat with a low pounding ripple, which slowly grew louder as Rafael joined in with the deep strains of his bass. Then Johnny raised the bow to his violin and slashed across the strings. The fans went wild, swaying to the rhythm of every stroke.

Finally it was Willow's turn. Roxy held her breath and hoped for the best.

Willow's fingers came down on the keys, producing the most gorgeous sound Roxy had ever heard. Music flowed from the piano like a living thing, wild and joyous and free. But Willow was obviously its master, her hands gliding across the keys with perfect control.

Roxy concentrated again on her drumming. Soon her part in the piece was over, and she had a few moments to relax while the others played.

She surveyed the audience again, picking out a few other familiar faces. She couldn't believe who she was seeing—it was Sneaky Pete, Jones and Face! They had come to the concert and were grooving to Johnny's new sound!

Roxy got an even bigger surprise when her gaze drifted to the back of the crowd. One man stood alone, away from everyone else. She gasped when she recognized him: the man with the mirrored shades!

Okay, Rox, relax, she told herself. *You've got a concert to perform. And anyway, that creep wouldn't dare attack us while we're onstage.* She picked up her drumsticks and waited for her cue. Then, beating the drums and clashing the cymbals, she somehow managed to get through the song—and the rest of the performance.

When the last piece ended, Roxy hopped to her feet and dashed across the stage. She had to warn Willow and the others.

"He's here! The man with the mirrored shades!" she shouted.

But it was useless. The audience was cheering so loudly the sound was almost deafening. Willow rose to the applause, throwing kisses to the crowd and bowing with Johnny Whisper.

Maybe if I point him out to her, Roxy thought, *she'll realize what danger she's in.*

But when Roxy looked back to the spot where she'd seen him, the man was gone. In a panic, she scanned the crowd and found him circling around the audience. He was pushing his way to the side of the stage.

And Willow was walking down the stairs—right into his grasp!

Roxy let out a scream. "Stop him! Somebody stop him!"

But the man grabbed Willow by the shoulders and gave her a big hug. A hug? Roxy couldn't believe it.

She dashed down the stage stairs. "Willow! Are you all right?"

"Yes," Willow said with a smile. "Gerald, meet Roxy. Roxy this is Gerald, my manager."

Roxy stared at Willow in shock. "Your what?"

"My manager," Willow repeated. "You see, Rox, I'm sort of a celebrity in the world of classical music. My name is Andrea Little."

"That's who you are!" Rafael exclaimed. "I knew I'd seen you somewhere. *Time* magazine did a cover story on you when you were only ten years old. They called you one of the greatest child prodigies since Mozart . . . and they predicted you could become one of the best concert pianists the world has ever seen!"

Willow blushed. "Those are just labels they slapped on me," she explained. "Do you know what it's like to be forced to do concerts and albums when you're only a teenager? Believe me, it's not fun. So, this week I took a little break and finally got to have fun. Thanks to you, Roxy."

Now it was Roxy's turn to blush. "Me?"

"Yeah. We both got to break out of the box and mix things up a bit, didn't we?"

Roxy smiled. It was true. The past week had been a real roller-coaster ride—and the greatest adventure of her life. *I guess I wasn't the only one on the ride*, she thought.

"So, have you had enough fun yet, Andrea?" Gerald butted in. "Are you ready to get back to work and finish that record we were making in New York?"

"Yes, Gerald. I'm ready, but I have to admit that making you chase me was a lot of fun, too," Andrea, the artist formerly known as Willow, said. She tilted her head. "But what do you think, Rox?" she asked. "Have we had enough fun yet?"

A second warehouse band burst into song on the stage.

"No way! I think we need to get in some serious dancing first," Roxy answered, grabbing her friend's hand and pulling her in front of the stage.

The girls burst out laughing and broke into a wild

dance, hopping and thrashing to the beat. Seconds later Rafael, Claire, and Betsy jumped into the mix.

Roxy glanced over to the side of the stage. Senator Darling shook Scratch's hand, and the Doll Heads slapped Johnny Whisper on the back. Everybody looked happy. Roxy was about to turn back to her friends when Johnny came dancing his way over to her.

"The Doll Heads aren't splitting up!" he shouted over the music. "The guys want to give it another shot!"

Roxy and Andrea cheered, giving Johnny a huge double hug.

He let out a victory yell and started jumping up and down. The whole audience was dancing now. Even Senator Darling grabbed the gray-haired receptionist and broke into a funky version of the twist!

Roxy twirled around to see Jane bopping around with Jason, the preppy punk. Laughing, she jumped in between them and mirrored her sister's moves. They giggled their way through the bump, the Watusi, and the moonwalk until Roxy broke away— and bumped into a tall man.

"I'm proud of you, Roxy."

She knew the voice, of course. She turned around to face her dad. He must have been telling the truth, because Roxy swore she'd never seen him look prouder.

"Hi, Dad." She hugged him tightly.

"You were great," Dr. Ryan said. "I never realized how serious you are about the drums . . . I guess what I mean is I get what you've been trying to tell me."

"Thanks, Dad. You're the best," Roxy replied.

At that moment the music changed to a slow song.

"Mind if I break in, Dr. Ryan?" Rafael held out a rose for Roxy.

Dr. Ryan stepped aside with a gracious smile.

Then, accepting the rose, Roxy took Rafael's hand and started to dance.

Maybe it was the music.

Maybe it was something in the air.

But Roxy had never been happier. She danced and smiled—and moved a little closer to Rafael.

So much for staying out of trouble, Roxy thought as he pulled her closer into his arms.

"This week was amazing," Rafael whispered. "Too bad you had to go through all that running around with the mirrored-shades guy."

Roxy thought about it. "Oh, I wouldn't change a thing," she told him.

"Really? Nothing?" Rafael asked, shaking his head.

"It was all great. Plus, tomorrow I go back to New York and get ready for my senior year—I don't think there is going to be a lot of running around the city and chasing bad guys and getting into trouble for me," Roxy said.

"Oh, I don't know," Rafael said. "There's something about you, Roxy. . . ."

"Something good?"

"Something great," he said as their lips met in a kiss—and it really was something!

Mary-Kate and Ashley's

GRADUATION SUMMER

is about to begin!

Senior prom, graduation, saying good-bye to old friends and making new ones. For Mary-Kate and Ashley, this is the summer that will change their lives forever . . . *Graduation Summer*. And they can't wait!

NEW

mary-kate and ashley

new york minute

We had our entire day planned... We thought! So how did we end up being chased all the way from Long Island through Chinatown to Harlem by police, politicians and an angry truant officer? We're still trying to figure it out!

Play out all your favorite scenes from *New York Minute* with our Mary-Kate and Ashley fashion dolls!

ONE WAY

ONE WAY

ONE WAY

Real Dolls for Real Girls

DUALSTAR CONSUMER PRODUCTS

MATTEL

Mary-Kate Olsen   Ashley Olsen

Experience the same hilarious trials and tribulations as Roxy and Jane did in their feature film *New York Minute*.

Bonus Movie
Mini-Poster!

www.mary-kateandashley.com

DUALSTAR
ONLINE

mary-kate olsen
ashley olsen
eugene levy
R
new york minute
In Theaters May 7th
www.newyorkminutemovie.com
WARNER BROS. PICTURES

Continue the

Adventure
in

New York Minute
*The Official Novelization
Based on the Big-Screen Movie*

and

**The Secret
of Jane's Success**